'So,' Angelo regarded her with those piercing black eyes, 'you managed to find your way to my room . . .'

Oh, lord, what was he thinking? 'I made a mistake,' Terri started to babble, not liking the way he was eyeing her now, his gaze travelling wantonly to her breasts, then downwards to caress her legs. 'It's not what you . . . I didn't mean to . . .' Dry-mouthed, she started to back away.

He smiled a strange smile. 'Don't apologise, *mia cara*. I'm not complaining.' Then he half turned round to lock the door, took the key carefully from the lock and dropped it into his jacket pocket. 'Though I have to say I'm a little surprised. I had no idea you'd be in such a hurry to do that market research we talked about.'

Terri opened her mouth to protest, but no sound came out. And suddenly her legs were rooted to the spot, paralysed with panic and horror, as on silent, panther-like strides he started to come across the room towards her.

Another book you will enjoy
by STEPHANIE HOWARD

BRIDE FOR A PRICE
As if her mother's death was not enough to cope with,
Olivia was shattered to discover that the family business
was now in the hands of arrogant Matthew Jordan. Olivia
was determined to reclaim it, but was she prepared to pay
the price Matthew demanded?

KISS OF THE FALCON

BY
STEPHANIE HOWARD

MILLS & BOON LIMITED
ETON HOUSE   18-24 PARADISE ROAD
RICHMOND   SURREY   TW9 1SR

All the characters in this book have no existence outside the imagination of the Author, and have no relation whatsoever to anyone bearing the same name or names. They are not even distantly inspired by any individual known or unknown to the Author, and all the incidents are pure invention.

All Rights Reserved. The text of this publication or any part thereof may not be reproduced or transmitted in any form or by any means, electronic or mechanical, including photocopying, recording, storage in an information retrieval system, or otherwise, without the written permission of the publisher.

This book is sold subject to the condition that it shall not, by way of trade or otherwise, be lent, resold, hired out or otherwise circulated without the prior consent of the publisher in any form of binding or cover other than that in which it is published and without a similar condition including this condition being imposed on the subsequent purchaser.

First published in Great Britain 1989
by Mills & Boon Limited

© Stephanie Howard 1989

Australian copyright 1989
Philippine copyright 1990
This edition 1990

ISBN 0 263 76519 9

Set in Plantin 11 on 12½ pt.
01 – 9001 – 48900

Typeset in Great Britain by JCL Graphics, Bristol

Made and Printed in Great Britain

CHAPTER ONE

THE motor-launch came shimmering out of the heat haze like a great white bird, slicing through the jewel-blue waters of the harbour as it headed for the jetty, twin sheets of foamy, iridescent spray arching outwards from its bows.

At the sight of it, Terri felt an apprehensive stab. So this was the 'taxi' that was to bear her to the falcon's nest and a confrontation she was starting to dread. She shook back her shoulder-length ash-blonde hair and firmed her lips in a resolute line. Nervous she might be, but she was determined to see her mission through. She hadn't just flown half-way across Europe to back out now.

'Eccolà, signorina! Venga! Follow me!' The skinny urchin in the faded T-shirt who had led her down from the cheap little *pensione* where she had spent the night, through the maze of steep, narrow streets to the island's noisy, throbbing harbour, was tugging impatiently at her skirt. 'Come!' he instructed. Then, with cries of *'Permesso! Permesso!'* he was steering a path for them through the crowd, his grubby face beaming importantly as men and women stood aside and heads turned curiously towards the slender, strikingly foreign-looking girl with the long blonde

hair and bright blue eyes.

Terri smiled wryly to herself. At least her mysteriously appointed guide seemed to be enjoying himself as they headed in single file towards the specially reserved mooring at the end of the jetty where the big, elegant motor-launch was already drawing in.

The boy grinned and gestured towards the vessel with its red and gold badge on the prow displaying the Montefalcone coat of arms. '*Ecco, signorina!* For you!' he proclaimed.

Terri grinned back at him as the irony of her situation occurred to her. In the face of this luxurious mode of transport that had suddenly been laid on for her, who would believe that, less than twenty-four hours ago, she had been struggling with her cases through the London Underground on her way to Victoria Coach Station and the cramped, crowded coach that was to take her to Luton airport to catch her flight to Sicily? Then, late last night, fighting her way through the steamy chaos of Catania to catch the last ferry south to Santa Pietrina?

It was all thanks to her sister Vicki that she was being treated so royally now. But then, it was only because of Vicki that she was here at all.

As the motor-launch bumped against the wooden jetty, she reached into her bag and handed the boy a handful of *lire*. '*Grazie*', she said with a smile. Then she turned to the bearded man in immaculate white shirt and ducks, the boat's co-pilot, who was addressing her now.

'Signorina Allan?' he enquired. Then, as Terri nodded, he told her, '*Venga a bordo*,' reaching out to offer her a steadying hand as she accepted his invitation and climbed aboard.

A moment later she was seated in the stern, the red leather of the upholstery hot from the sun against her back, the warm wind whipping through her hair as the boat wheeled in a wide arc round the harbour and headed back for the open sea. From here, it was a fast fifteen-minute ride round to the more secluded south side of the island and the aptly named Casa Grande where the Marchese Angelo de Montefalcone resided. And where she was headed now. 'This is it, Vicki,' she muttered under her breath. 'Now, let's just pray that I can deliver the goods.'

She swivelled round in her seat to gaze towards the fast-receding shoreline, a narrow ribbon of silver glistening beneath the scorching July sun. Behind it, the ochre-walled, red-roofed buildings of the little town, and beyond, the cypress-fringed, hilly interior of the island, dominated by the craggy Monte Falcone. Falcon Mountain. Mysterious and slightly forbidding, just like its name.

Terri turned away. The last and only time she had visited the island had been for her sister's wedding three years ago—when Vicki had somewhat astounded her family by becoming sister-in-law to an Italian marquis. Though that was not strictly true, Terri reminded herself. Ruggero, Vicki's husband, was actually only Angelo's cousin, though they had been brought up like brothers from childhood, since the death of Ruggero's parents.

At any rate, Vicki appeared to have been living like a

jet-set member of the aristocracy for the past three years. In her infrequent letters, she had described to Terri the hectic round of partying and globe-trotting that had apparently left her no time even for the occasional visit home. Then had come the birth of her daughter Laura eighteen months ago, and Vicki's life had seemed doubly blessed.

Stuck in the predictable routine of a temporary secretary's life in London, Terri had often thought of her little sister living on her sun-drenched Mediterranean island with her handsome husband and little daughter and had secretly envied her. So it had come as a total shock when Vicki had turned up right out of the blue at her Kentish Town flat a couple of nights ago, distraught and tearful, and announced that her marriage was on the rocks.

Terri had stared at her in disbelief. 'But why? What's happened?' she'd wanted to know.

Vicki had sunk down on a chair and blinked across at her through tear-filled eyes. 'We've had the most terrible row. Ruggero's gone off.' Her face crumpled. 'And he's taken Laura.' Terri had knelt at her feet as she went on through her sobs, 'It's all their fault. They've always hated me—and now they've turned Ruggero against me!'

'Who, Vicki? Who's turned Ruggero against you?'

'All of them. The whole damned Montefalcone clan. But especially Angelo.' Vicki sniffed and pushed back a strand of short-cropped hair. 'He runs Ruggero's life for him as though he were a child, and Ruggero lets him. And he tries to interfere in every little thing I do. He's destroyed our marriage. It's over, Terri.'

Terri frowned. 'Was that what the row was about?'

Dumbly, Vicki nodded. 'I told Ruggero I couldn't stand it any more. I threatened to leave him and come back to England with Laura—and the next thing I knew, he'd disappeared.' Her face crumpled again. 'He's taken my baby,' she wailed. 'Please help me to get my baby back!'

Terri took her hand to comfort her. 'Where has he taken her? Do you know?'

Vicki's lips trembled. She shook her head. 'No, but I know who will. Angelo.' Her mouth twisted as she spoke the name. 'There's not a leaf falls on that island without Angelo knowing about it. He'll know where Ruggero's taken her.'

'Have you spoken to him?'

She made a face. 'There's no point in that. He hates me, Terri. Almost as much as I hate him. It would be a waste of time for me to try to get anything out of him.' A sudden light came into her eyes. 'But you could, Terri, I know you could. You could persuade him to listen to you.'

'Me? I don't even know the man!'

'Please, Terri, do this for me. For me and baby Laura. For your niece. Go to the island and speak to him. Persuade him to tell Ruggero to give my baby back to me. Ruggero will do anything that Angelo says.' Tears streamed down her face as she pleaded, 'Please, Terri! I'll never in all my life ask you to do anything for me again.'

Less than forty-eight hours later, Terri had been on

her way. How could she turn down such a plea? Besides, looking after Vicki was second nature to her. Though less than three years separated them, she had always been the one that little sister Vicki turned to when she was in a jam.

The motor-launch was wheeling round towards the shore again. Terri shaded her eyes with her hand and squinted up at the sprawling, majestic lines of the Casa Grande perched high on the cliff, its domes and turrets and high, secluding walls lending it the mysterious air of some Moorish stronghold of old. She had seen it before on her previous visit, but she had never set foot inside. And she had not been exaggerating when she had protested to Vicki that its owner was virtually a total stranger to her. She had been introduced to the Marchese briefly at the wedding, and she had a strong, sharp memory of a dark, forbidding presence. But that was as far as their acquaintanceship went.

As the shoreline loomed closer, the knot of anxiety inside her tightened. In spite of her determination to stand by Vicki, she was not looking forward to what lay ahead. If Angelo was even half the monster that Vicki had painted him, this meeting, at best, would be difficult. It could be an outright ordeal at the worst.

They docked at the private marina, then Terri was led across sun-scorched cobblestones to an elevator shaft hewn from the cliff-face, where an elderly manservant in black trousers and a blue jacket was waiting for her.

'Now you go with him,' her bearded escort instructed her in heavily accented English—and she barely had time to offer him a courteous nod of thanks before she found herself being ushered into the cool interior of the lift. Then the grille doors closed and she and her silent companion were being borne aloft, swiftly and soundlessly, through the living rock.

A moment later the doors opened again and Terri blinked in wondering astonishment as the man in the crisp blue jacket stepped aside to allow her to pass ahead of him into a huge, high-ceilinged hall, divided into two by tall, sweeping arches and hung with intricately worked brass lamps. She had been expecting to emerge in some outer courtyard, not right in the heart of the Montefalcone residence.

'*Momento, signorina. Aspetti qua.*' With a brief bow and a wave of his hand, the man indicated one of the elaborately carved, deep-cushioned divans that were ranged against the blue and white tiled walls. Obediently she sat, feeling the silk brocade of the cushions cool against her back, and watched as the man padded off through one of the archways to some hidden inner sanctum beyond.

Into whose hands would she be delivered next? she wondered wryly to herself, smoothing her slim skirt over her thighs and shaking back her loose blonde hair. From early this morning, when she had made her first attempt to contact Angelo, she had been passed from hand to hand like a parcel. First she had spoken on the phone to some unidentified member of the Montefalcone entourage, then waited over an hour in the stifling heat of the *pensione* for that same person to call back with a message from his master that she should present herself at the harbour in half an hour's time. Then, just as she was about to seek directions from the *padrona* behind the desk, the urchin in the faded T-shirt had materialised like a shadow from off the wall. 'Signorina Allan? Come, please, with me.'

It wouldn't surprise her in the least if yet another anonymous lackey were to appear like a genie before her now and spirit her off somewhere else.

'Welcome to Casa Grande. It is my unexpected pleasure to receive you at my home.'

The man who had appeared soundlessly through the archway was no lackey. As Terri glanced up at him with a start, she saw a tall, broad-shouldered figure in an immaculate pale linen suit, the forceful features deeply bronzed. Straight nose, wide mouth, a high, smooth brow. And a head of collar-length hair as black and glossy as washed coal.

She had been right to remember him as forbidding. In spite of the faint smile of welcome that hovered around his lips, Angelo de Montefalcone carried about him an aura of uncompromising authority that was vaguely unsettling. As he came towards her, one hand extended in greeting, she rose to her feet. 'Thank you,' she murmured.

The clasp of his hand was firm and cool, the eyes that met hers as dark as midnight. 'This is indeed a surprise. What brings you to Santa Pietrina?' he enquired. 'Are you here on holiday?'

'Not exactly.' She forced herself to hold his gaze. 'As a matter of fact, I've come to see you.'

One straight black eyebrow lifted at her. 'All this way, just to see me?' An amused, faintly mocking smile flitted across his face. 'In that case,' he told her in a deep, velvet voice, 'let us make ourselves more comfortable.'

He led her into a large, airy room, half shuttered against the fierce midday light. A study of some description, Terri deduced, observing the large, paper-strewn desk by the window—and she wondered vaguely if this were some deliberately calculated insult on his part that he should receive her in the semi-formal surroundings of a work-place rather than in the more intimate confines of his private living-quarters. No matter, she thought brusquely to herself. She had not come to be sociable.

At least he did not seat himself behind the desk, but crossed to a low, square table in one corner, flanked on two sides by deep divans. 'Be seated,' he invited with a wave of his hand, then waited politely till she had done so before lowering his tall frame against the cushions of the divan opposite.

A man appeared in the doorway, carrying a tray. 'Iced tea,' Angelo informed her as the man laid out tall glasses in pierced silver holders on the table in front of them and poured the amber liquid, sprigged with leaves of fresh mint, from a matching silver-encased jug. 'In this warm weather, it is very refreshing.'

It was. Terri drank gratefully, resisting the urge to gulp it down. The unaccustomed heat, added to her apprehension, had made her mouth quite dry. She glanced over the rim of her glass at the cool figure seated opposite. Somehow she could not imagine this man ever being apprehensive about anything—nor less than totally in control of any situation.

He was leaning lightly against the cushions at his back, one arm stretched out along the back of the divan, the cuff of his jacket shot back slightly to reveal a strong, brown wrist, a well-shaped hand. Casually he hooked the ankle of one leg over the opposite knee, causing the expensively tailored cloth to tauten against one lean and powerfully sinewed thigh. Terri glanced across at the handmade shoes, discreet cream shirt and pale silk tie and, suddenly feeling his eyes on her, was acutely conscious of her own attire.

'Wear something sexy,' Vicki had advised. 'If the impenetrable Angelo has one weakness, it's his predilection for good-looking women.'

Hence the figure-hugging, thigh-high skirt and the skimpy halter-top she had chosen. Not her usual style at all—and an error of judgement, she sensed now. A man like Angelo de Montefalcone would not be tempted by such obvious bait.

All the same, she was aware of the dark gaze roaming insolently over her imprudently exposed flesh—the slender calves and thighs and shapely shoulders—then pausing to graze the thinly clad, small, pointed breasts, as he prompted with a superior smile, 'So what's your business—since you say you're not here on holiday?'

It wasn't the friendliest opening she could have hoped for. Terri laid down her glass. 'I may extend my visit into a holiday.' If all went well, she'd promised herself a well-deserved couple of weeks at some resort on mainland Italy. 'But no. As I told you, that's not why I'm here.'

He raised one curious eyebrow at her. 'You've come to see me, if I understand right.'

She nodded as the dark eyes scrutinised her face. And, in spite of his easy manner, she could sense the hostility in him. He knew exactly why she had come, but, for whatever reasons of his own, he was out to make her task as difficult as possible. She cleared her throat and came straight to the point. 'I've come here to talk about Vicki, in fact.'

'Vicki?' There was surprise in his voice.

'My sister.'

He smiled a condescending smile. 'I do know who she is. She is married to my cousin, remember?' With a twist of his lips, he managed to convey that this fact was not entirely pleasing to him. He reached out and picked up his untouched glass, then raised it slowly to his lips. 'However, I'm afraid you've rather mistimed your visit. She left the island some days ago.'

He was playing some game with her. Warding her off. Every time she took a step forward, he managed to push her two steps back. Terri straightened in her seat and looked across at him levelly. 'I know that,' she said. 'She's been staying with me in London for the past two days. I didn't come here to see Vicki. I came to speak to you.' She took a deep breath and plunged on quickly before he could trip her up again. 'I understand that Ruggero has taken Laura away.'

'Is that so?' One black eyebrow lifted, as though this information was news to him. He drank slowly from his glass, then laid it on the table again. 'And what is so unusual about that? He is the child's father, after all.' He smiled. 'And someone has to look after his daughter while his wife is off enjoying herself in London.'

For a moment she was uncertain whether the veiled note in his voice was cool detachment or simple derision—though it was hard to believe there could be anything simple about the Marchese de Montefalcone. He was a man, she had already deduced, whose instincts would be as ruthless and as calculating as the bird of prey whose name he bore. It was becoming more and more easy to understand why Vicki detested him as she did.

She explained, allowing room for doubt. 'I don't think you've understood. It isn't a simple case of Ruggero looking after the child. He's snatched her. He and Vicki have had a quarrel. The marriage is over. And my sister wants her daughter back.'

Cool eyes met hers. 'That sounds a little melodramatic to me. Quarrels are not uncommon between spouses. Surely it's jumping the gun a bit to suggest that the marriage is over?'

'Not according to my sister. She says it's definitely finished.' Terri refrained from elaborating on the part he himself had played in bringing about this sad state of affairs. For the moment, at any rate, she needed to have him on her side. She repeated what she'd said before. 'And Vicki wants her daughter back.'

For a moment he said nothing, just continued to regard her through openly censorious jet-black eyes. 'So why have you come to me?' he asked at last.

'Vicki thinks you might know where Ruggero is—and that you might be able to persuade him to give Laura back to her.'

This time there was no mistaking the note of derision in his voice. 'Does she really?' he enquired. 'Then why didn't she tackle me herself, instead of flying off to London and sending you here in her place?'

Terri decided to level with him. 'Because she thought you would be more likely to listen to me.' She held his eyes and added anxiously, 'My sister is extremely upset—as you would expect. She desperately wants her daughter back.'

He made an impatient gesture. 'I am most touched, I assure you.' His tone was harshly cynical, belying the sentiment. 'But I'm afraid your journey has been a waste of time. I have no idea where my cousin is.'

'Are you sure?'

'Are you calling me a liar?'

She glanced away. At least, to his face, she would never dare to call him that.

'Good,' he warned her. 'That would be most unwise.'

Terri composed herself. 'But surely it would be within your powers to locate him if you wanted to?'

'And why should I want to?'

'I've told you—he's taken Laura. He has no right to do that.'

'He has every right.' The black eyes held hers. 'He is the child's father, as I keep reminding you.'

His total intransigence was starting to grate on

Terri's nerves. Trying to reason with him was like butting one's head against a wall. But, for Vicki's sake, she kept her temper and made another try. 'And doesn't a mother have the right of access to her child? Vicki doesn't even know where Laura is!'

'Does she think the child is in London?'

The question surprised her. 'No,' she replied.

'So why, if your sister is so concerned about her daughter's whereabouts, has she gone there?'

'I told you—she's very upset. She flew to London to persuade me to come and talk to you.' On an impulse, she added for good measure, 'And, I dare say, to take legal advice.'

Angelo ran one sun-browned finger lightly over his chin, and dismissed the veiled threat with a scoffing laugh. 'That would indeed be a pointless exercise. Permit me to remind you that the child is an Italian citizen, born in Italy of an Italian father and a mother whose official residence for the past several years has also been in Italy.' He threw her a scathing smile. 'I fail to see what useful assistance an English court could possibly provide.'

With a faint lift of triumph, Terri pounced on him. 'So you admit that Ruggero has snatched the child?'

'Admit?' But he was not so easily outflanked. 'It is not I who am in any way on trial here. Whatever dispute may exist is between my cousin and your sister. It is up to them to settle it in whatever way they see fit.'

'Then you refuse to help?'

'That is correct.' He threw her a contemptuous look

and rose abruptly to his feet. 'This is a private, family matter. It is not up to me to interfere.'

What he was really saying, of course, was that it was *his* family's business and that *she* was the one who should not interfere. Riled at his arrogance, she suddenly couldn't resist pointing out, 'According to my sister, that isn't your usual line. She tells me it's your normal practice to interfere rather a lot.'

'Does she?' He was standing over her, hands thrust deep into the pockets of his trousers, the black eyes narrowed menacingly as he frowned down at her. 'Then it would appear that your sister has a remarkable talent for distorting the truth. If I had wished to interfere, she would have been gone from here long ago.' With a final crushing glance, he turned away. 'I would advise you not to take too seriously her tales of persecution. I fear she is something of a liar.'

Terri glared at him. 'Well, there's one thing I can assure you—she told the absolute truth about you!'

The Marchese ignored the remark and crossed to the window, then stood with his back to her, staring outside. Without turning, he informed her, 'I think we have exhausted the subject. I would suggest now that you go back to your hotel, pack your bags and arrange to catch the first flight from Sicily back to London.' Before she could answer, he half turned round, so that his features were in profile against the light, the forceful, vivid lines of the straight brow and nose, the firm, hard mouth, the aggressive chin. 'There is really nothing to detain you here.'

She flinched slightly. 'Are you throwing me off the island?' she asked.

He smiled. 'Would I be so uncivil?' He dismissed the very notion with a disdainful shrug. 'No, I am merely pointing out to you, in case you have failed to see it for yourself, that your little mission of mercy has foundered. I assure you it would be a waste of time for you to consider staying on.'

Terri tilted her chin at him defiantly. 'That has still to be seen. Perhaps you're not the only person on this island who can help me. And others may prove more co-operative than you.'

The fine lips tightened—a warning signal. And a flash of anger lit the dark eyes. Terri felt her stomach tighten as he turned head on to look at her. Suddenly he looked dangerous. But, at the last minute, he seemed to pull himself back. He gave an elaborate shrug. 'Suit yourself,' he said. Then, with renewed composure, he glanced down quickly at the slim gold watch at his wrist. 'I generally have lunch about now. You may join me, if you have no other plans.'

It was hardly the most pressing invitation she had ever received. Only a deep-bred sense of chivalry had prompted him to issue it at all, and she could tell it would suit him nicely if she were to decline. For her own part, she had not the slightest desire to spend a moment longer in his company.

But her personal feelings were not her most urgent consideration right now. For Vicki's sake, she had to keep trying. And, besides, she had obviously touched a sensitive spot with her threat to seek help elsewhere on the island. The Marchese would not like that. Outsiders being involved in family business was not something he would lightly tolerate. Perhaps, she decided, she could use that threat to manipulate him into co-operating with her. It was a long shot. But it was worth a try.

She threw him a stiff smile. 'I have no other plans. I'd be delighted to join you for lunch.'

She watched through lowered lashes as he reached for the phone on the desk and spoke in rapid Italian into it. Angelo de Montefalcone, she sensed, was a complex and ruthless man. No pampered, soft aristocrat, despite the ancient title he bore. No wonder, while the bulk of Europe's displaced nobility were repining in genteel poverty these days, this man, even now barely thirty-four years old, had built himself a shipping empire that had brought the Montefalcone name more wealth and power than his forebears had ever dreamed of. It was really hardly surprising that he was proving such a tough adversary.

He laid down the phone and turned to her. 'Ten minutes. We can have an *aperitivo* while we wait.' As she nodded assent and got to her feet, he crossed to a door on the far side of the room and stood politely aside to let her pass ahead of him into the smaller room beyond. 'I often eat here when I'm working,' he told her. 'I hope you'll forgive the informality.'

A small table, already set for two, stood by the open veranda doors, with a magnificent view out over the bay. So her acceptance of his invitation to lunch had been presumed even before the invitation had been made! With a twist of irritation, Terri glanced round. The pale linen cloth, gleaming silver and long-stemmed glasses were not what she herself would have called informal. Nor was the tasteful, elegant décor of the rest of the room. She found herself wondering, faintly intrigued, what in Angelo's book would qualify as grand.

He moved to the cabinet against one wall, where a battery of bottles were discreetly arranged. She watched as he half filled two glasses with ice and poured a generous measure of some mysterious dark gold liquid into each of them. 'A local *amaro*,' he told her, handing one of the glasses to her. 'I hope it's to your taste.'

She nodded agreeably. It was bitter, as its name suggested, but not unpleasant. An acquired taste.

Angelo took an appreciative mouthful of his. 'So tell me,' he enquired conversationally, 'when did you arrive on the island?'

'Last night.'

'And where did you spend the night?'

'At the Pensione Rosa.'

He raised an eyebrow in surprise. 'Rather a spartan establishment, is it not?'

Of course, he would think so—and it was a far cry from the four-star Hotel Mediterraneo where Vicki and Ruggero's reception had been held. She frowned back at him. 'It's perfectly adequate for my needs.'

He threw her a curious glance. 'I would have thought your fiancé could have stretched to a little better than that.'

Fiancé? The word sent an odd sensation down her spine. She had almost forgotten that Steve had accompanied her to the wedding—and she had certainly not expected Angelo to recall such a detail. She sighed inwardly. How long ago it had been! Steve and all that part of her life seemed now like a world away. Abruptly, she answered, 'Steve and I are no longer engaged. I came here alone.'

'I see.' He regarded her closely with those piercing dark eyes. 'So the engagement was dissolved?'

Awkwardly, Terri dropped her gaze, not wishing to pursue the subject. 'Over a year ago.' On her twenty-third birthday, to be precise.

The eyebrow lifted. 'The novelty began to pall, no doubt. You felt the need to move on and experiment with pastures new.'

In the sudden oasis of civility, his harsh tone caught her unawares. She glanced up, feeling the heat rise to her cheeks as the dark eyes swept over her from head to toe, stripping her naked where she stood, seeming to ravish her in a single glance, then cast her contemptuously aside. Momentarily too taken aback to defend herself properly, she answered almost apologetically, 'The relationship ended, that's all.'

He threw her a disparaging look. 'You English take your commitments so lightly, of course.'

At that, something inside her snapped. He was wrong and he had no right to speak to her like that. Her fingers tightened around her glass. Her eyes glared back at him with intense dislike. 'And you and

your kind are nothing but two-faced hypocrites!'
she spat. 'You pretend to care so much about your
family, but it's all rather different when you're
put to the test. When a helpless eighteen-month-
old child is kidnapped and taken from her mother,
you show no more concern than if it were a
dog!'

The expression on Angelo's face had darkened
dangerously. The wide mouth tightened, the lines
around his jaw grew hard.

But Terri was not about to be intimidated into
stopping in midstream. Her anger was not easily
aroused, but he had gone too far. 'That is why,' she
hurried on, biting out each word at him, 'with or
without your co-operation, I intend to find my niece
and take her back to England, where there are people
who genuinely care for her!'

He took a step forward. 'That will never happen!'
He loomed over her threateningly. 'Never! You can
take my word for it.'

She stood her ground. 'Oh yes, it will!'

'No, *cara*. Never!' He was standing so close to her
now that she could feel the heat of anger in him. It
seemed to rage at her from every sinew of his tall,
powerful frame. Yet a curious chill went through her
as she met his eyes—cruel, dark, uncompromising
bayonets of steel.

'And shall I tell you why?' he demanded, then
continued with venom as she backed away, 'Because,
mia cara, I shall personally see to it that that
child, blood of my blood, will die before I will allow

her to be delivered into the hands of a family of whores!'

CHAPTER TWO

IT WAS as though he had struck her. With a gasp of
protest, Terri reeled back away from him, her cheeks
pale with indignation, a dazed and deeply offended
expression on her face.

'How dare you——?' she began. But, just at that
moment, she was interrupted as a door opened silently
and a uniformed servant entered the room pushing a
trolley laden with covered silver dishes and a bottle of
white wine cooling in a bucket of ice.

'Ah, lunch has arrived.' As calmly as though he and
his guest had just been discussing the weather, Angelo
waved towards the little table that stood by the open
veranda doors. 'Shall we be seated?' he invited with a
caustic smile.

In an effort to control her anger, Terri clenched her
fists. Inside, she was trembling violently. She felt
numb with outrage, slightly sick. She glared with a
sudden fierce loathing at the composed, dark figure in
the pale linen suit. A family of whores, he had said.
What on earth had he meant by that?

With elaborate politeness, he pulled back her chair
for her. '*Prego*. Allow me.' And Terri only just
managed to smother the impulse to turn right round
and walk out the door. She couldn't do that. For

26

Vicki's sake. She sat down stiffly, avoiding his eyes.

'Thank you,' she shot back sarcastically.

With a flourish, the man in the waiter's uniform removed the lid from one of the silver salvers. '*Frutti di mare*,' he announced, revealing a concoction of mussels, giant prawns and succulent lobster tails, all done up in a tangy garlic and tomato sauce. '*Pescati stamani*,' he added, offering the dish to Terri. And, with a gallant smile, Angelo translated for his guest.

'He's telling you that our lunch was caught earlier this morning.' He shook his linen napkin across his lap as the man moved round the table to serve him. 'The waters around the island keep us well-supplied. What with that and the produce from our farms, foodwise, we're virtually self-sufficient.'

Terri forced herself to look at him and offered a dry smile in response. Self-sufficiency was one attribute she had no difficulty whatsoever in associating with him. On the contrary. Like his namesake, the falcon, he would fly alone, a single-minded, ruthless provider for his own needs. She threw him a false smile. 'How nice for you,' she said.

Amusement flickered across his face. 'Yes, I admit I do find it rather gratifying.' Then, as the waiter poured the wine, 'Eat,' he instructed, and waved the man away with a murmured, '*Grazie. Va bene così*.'

But eat was the last thing she felt able to do. In spite of her calm exterior, her stomach was churning and

her mouth felt dry. Motionless, she stared at her plate
and waited till the man had left the room. Then,
slowly, she raised her eyes to Angelo. In a cold voice,
she told him, 'Now I would be grateful if you would
explain that remark.'

He deftly extricated a mussel from its shell and met
her eyes with feigned ignorance. 'And which
particular remark might you be referring to?' he
asked.

'You know very well which remark I'm referring
to.' She narrowed her eyes at him, disdaining to sully
her lips by repeating his monstrous calumny. 'I'd like
you to explain exactly what you meant by it.'

He chewed the mussel thoughtfully and washed it
down with a mouthful of wine. 'I wouldn't have
thought that was something that needed much
clarification,' he said at last. 'I was referring to your
sister.' The black eyes held hers without remorse.
'Your sister is a whore—or didn't you know?'

Indignation drained the colour from Terri's cheeks.
So he had the gall to say it again! She glared
ferociously across the table at him, resisting the
almost overwhelming urge to throw the contents of
her wineglass in his face. 'That's a filthy thing to say!
And a lie!' she accused. 'What right do you have to say
something like that?'

He shrugged broad shoulders. 'The right of one
who has observed certain aspects of her behaviour and
come to the obvious conclusion,' he said.

He was so matter-of-fact, and that somehow only
sharpened the insult. Angrily Terri challenged him,

'And what exactly have you observed?'

He leaned back in his chair. 'A great deal,' he assured her. 'And none of it to my liking, I may say. Even before she married Ruggero, that first summer she spent on Santa Pietrina, I could tell what type of girl she was.' Disapproval tugged at his lip. 'She is the type of female, *mia cara*, for whom the attentions of one man are never enough. She craves constant admiration and flattery from every man who crosses her path. I warned Ruggero, but to no avail.'

So he had started his interfering early, Terri thought bitterly to herself. Poor Vicki hadn't really stood a chance. Her chin firmed defensively. 'What you're saying is ridiculous. My sister may be a bit of a flirt——' Vicki had always attracted male attentions '—but that's harmless. It certainly doesn't make her into what you're accusing her of being!'

'That may be,' he conceded. 'Flirtation, as you so rightly say, is generally a harmless pursuit.' A look that was at once amused and provocative flashed across the deep, dark eyes. As he scanned her face, Terri was suddenly aware of a strange pulse throbbing in her throat, a tingle shooting across her scalp, making the hairs on the back of her neck stand up. Hurriedly she dropped her eyes as Angelo went on, 'Flirtation is part of the complex, unspoken language that passes constantly between the sexes. And not only is it mostly harmless, it can be thoroughly enjoyable. All of us indulge in it from time to time.'

She swallowed. 'So why are you being so hard on Vicki?'

'Because with Vicki it did not end there.'

'And what does that insinuation mean?'

He sighed and ran long, tanned fingers thoughtfully across his chin. 'As you know, my cousin works for me. At times, his duties take him away from Santa Pietrina—often to the mainland and frequently abroad. Before their daughter was born, your sister generally accompanied him, but later that was not always possible. Your sister resented that. She did not enjoy being left at home.' He toyed with his cutlery. 'Let's just say that in the absence of her husband, she found other ways of amusing herself.'

Terri glared at him. She didn't like what he had just implied. 'You mean she had the effrontery to pursue some kind of social life, even when Ruggero was away? What did you expect her to do? Sit at home and polish the silver all day?'

An amused smile curved around the well-shaped lips. 'I doubt very much that your sister was ever required to perform such menial manual labour while she was here. However, I take your point. I would not expect her to cloister herself like a nun during her husband's absences.' Then a harsh look replaced the momentary humour in his eyes as he deliberately focused on her face. 'Nor would I expect her to be seen in public with other men, nor to entertain them overnight at her home.'

Terri blanched, genuinely shocked. Were there no depths to which he would not sink in order to blacken her sister's name? She stared back at him levelly. 'I don't believe you,' she said.

'That, of course, is your privilege.' With a dismissive flick of his eyes, Angelo sat forward in his seat and applied himself once more to the food on his plate. 'I have explained to you the reason why I called your sister a whore and why I am ill-disposed to assist you in your efforts to return her daughter to her.' He nodded brusquely towards her own untouched plate. 'I would suggest you drop the subject now and eat. Seafood is not so tasty when it is eaten cold.'

Whatever appetite Terri might once have had had completely disappeared. In impotent anger, she stared across at him. 'I should have known,' she accused bitterly, 'that you would close ranks with Ruggero over this. Vicki told me what you were like. But let me tell you, I don't believe a single word of anything you've just said about Vicki. You're just making it up to try and justify keeping her daughter from her!'

'I am making nothing up. Believe me, I would not waste my powers of invention on someone like your sister.'

She threw him a harsh look. 'How can you side with a man who spirits away his daughter like that? Surely even you can see it's a despicable thing to do?'

He regarded her steadily. 'Despicable? I would not call it so. On the contrary, I would say that any man who makes the discovery that his wife is behaving like a tramp is perfectly entitled to remove their child.'

'So that's what you're suggesting? That Ruggero found out about Vicki's supposed misdemeanours and removed the child for her own good?' A look of unbridled contempt crossed her face. 'Did you tell him these lies—as part of your campaign to turn him against her?'

Angelo gave a light, sarcastic laugh. 'As I have already told you, it is your sister who is the liar. I gather now from this talk of campaigns that she is also somewhat paranoid.'

Terri glowered at him, ignoring that last obfuscatory remark. She told him, 'According to Vicki, you have a great deal of influence over Ruggero. He would believe anything you said.' Then she couldn't resist adding, vindictively, 'He sounds a little weak to me.' It was not, after all, Angelo's exclusive prerogative to insult other people's next of kin. She went on, warming to her self-appointed task, 'Vicki should never have married him. She needs someone strong.'

He smiled. 'To keep her in line, you mean?'

She scowled across at him. 'No, I didn't mean that!' Though it was precisely the sort of chauvinistic remark she would have expected him to make. 'My sister needs someone she can lean on. Ruggero doesn't have it in him to measure up.'

The black eyes swept over her, an unfathomable expression in their smoky depths. Then he told her, 'It would appear that in certain departments you and your sister are somewhat difficult to please.'

The oblique allusion to her broken engagement was not hard to detect. With her eyes, she dared him to pursue the subject. What had passed between herself and Steve was intensely private—and it still hurt. And Angelo had no right at all to pass judgement on her for it.

Apparently, for the moment, he had no interest in doing so anyway. Returning to the subject of Ruggero, he put to her, 'Whatever your private opinion of him as a husband may be, you cannot deny that he's a good father.'

A doting father, according to her sister's reports. At least she had no fears that while the child was with Ruggero she would be in safe and caring hands. 'That's not the point,' she insisted stubbornly. 'He had no right to take Laura from her mother.'

He eyed her censoriously. 'Forgive me,' he said with sarcasm in his voice, 'I would have thought that was precisely the point. Surely the welfare of the child is of paramount importance?'

Terri frowned at him. 'Of course it is,' she defended. 'But her welfare would be equally assured with Vicki. That's why I intend to get her back.'

He made a weary gesture. 'I think there is no further point in discussing this subject. You are free to do whatever you wish. Just don't expect any assistance from me.'

'I shall manage without it. As I've already told you, I don't intend to restrict my enquiries to you. Perhaps there are some people on this island who don't approve as wholeheartedly of kidnapping as you appear to do.'

For a moment he said nothing, but a dark warning shone deep in his eyes. 'Tread very carefully, *mia cara*,' he advised.

The subject was dropped. For the moment, there was clearly nothing to be gained by pursuing it. And much to be lost, she sensed, by deliberately antagonising this man. If she had hoped to manoeuvre him into a corner by threatening to ask around, she could see now just how foolish that notion had been. Angelo de Montefalcone was unmanoeuvrable. All she would accomplish by arousing his hostility would be to make her task even more difficult.

As they ate and she followed his adroit lead into more neutral conversational waters, Terri eyed him surreptitiously through lowered lids. He had refused to help her, but at least he had said she could do as she wished. Perhaps, if she were discreet, he would not try to hamper her investigations. So she would be discreet. At all costs, she must not jeopardise what little advantage she had left.

When the coffee was brought, Angelo suggested that they take it outside. 'If it's not too hot for you out there.'

'No, I would like that,' she assured him, as the servant led her on to the veranda where some white-painted chairs and a table were arranged. As Angelo sat down in one of the chairs, his long legs stretched out casually in front of him, she crossed to the parapet and leaned against it, enjoying the caress of the warm sea breeze as it ruffled her loose blonde hair. With a sigh, she let her gaze sweep round the magnificent clear blue of the bay to the eastern side of the island where she could just glimpse the outline of the island's rocky interior. Falcon Mountain. She narrowed her eyes and enquired over her shoulder, 'Are there really falcons on the mountain? Is that how it got its name?'

She heard the click of a coffee-cup against a saucer. 'Once upon a time, there used to be many. Now, like so many species around the world, the falcon is threatened.' A pause. 'But we take care to guard the ones that are left. It would be a tragedy if the island were to lose one of its oldest and most noble inhabitants.'

'What do you mean when you say you guard them?' She half turned round suspiciously. 'Don't tell me you keep the birds in captivity?'

'Some.' As the blue eyes locked with his own, Angelo seemed to smile a challenge at her. 'In their own interests, you understand. We have a number that are kept for breeding purposes. The chicks are then released back into the wild.' He raised one dark eyebrow at her. 'It is not so terrible for them. In spite of their inherent wildness, they have a long and close association with man.'

'In hunting, you mean?'

'The bond between a well-trained falcon and its master is a remarkable one. And one that goes back thousands of years.'

She threw him a disapproving look. 'I've always thought it a rather cruel sport.'

He smiled. 'It is cruel only in so far as nature herself is cruel. The falcon is a natural hunter which only kills its natural prey. And it is a swift and efficient killer. The fatal blow has been struck before the prey is even aware of the danger it is in.'

As the black eyes swept her face, Terri felt a little inward shiver. Abruptly, she turned away. It was almost as though he had been warning her.

There was a silence. Terri kept her back to him, fighting to quell the sudden strange fluttering in her heart. Then he told her, glancing down unhurriedly at his watch. 'If you will forgive me, it is getting late. I have certain business matters to attend to that will not wait.' As she turned round to look at him, unblinking black eyes met hers. 'As soon as you have finished your coffee, I shall arrange for you to be accompanied back to your hotel.' He reached out to pick up the cordless phone that lay on the tabletop in front of him, and added carefully, still watching her, 'Let me repeat the advice I have already given you. Waste no more time on the island. Just pack your bags, return to Catania and book a seat on the first available flight back to England. You will achieve nothing by staying on here.'

She threw him a defiant look. 'We shall see,' she retorted.

'Indeed we shall.' He smiled a harsh smile and kept his gaze fixed threateningly on her as he spoke quickly into the phone. Then, as he laid it down again, he observed, 'Besides, I hardly think it advisable for a young woman of your charms to be here unaccompanied.'

Terri dismissed the notion. 'Don't worry about me. I shall come to no harm. I'm perfectly used to looking after myself.'

'Perhaps.' Slowly he got to his feet. 'But remember, this is not England, *mia cara*. A young woman as conspicuous as yourself may attract unwanted attentions.' Then he added pointedly, his eyes sweeping over her scanty attire, 'Unless, of course, like your sister, you have a taste for casual sexual adventures.'

With perfect timing, before she could retaliate, the man in the blue and black uniform who had accompanied her from the lift appeared in the veranda doorway.

Angelo extended one hand to her. '*Addio*,' he told her, clasping hers briefly. '*Bon voyage*.'

Seething, Terri grabbed her bag. All the things that Vicki had told her about him were true. Only he was a hundred times worse. He was an insufferable, arrogant, chauvinistic bully without one redeeeming feature to his name. She stalked on stiff legs behind the blue uniform through the study to the door that led out to the hall, suddenly anxious to escape from this hostile place.

Aware that Angelo had followed her, she paused at the door and flung sarcastically over her shoulder, 'Thank you for your *memorable* hospitality!'

But, before the door closed, he had the final word.

'The last ferry to the mainland leaves at midnight. Be sure you're on it,' he said.

She was not on it.

Earlier in the evening, she had phoned Vicki. 'Not much progress so far,' she'd admitted, anxious not to upset her sister by revealing how bad things really were.

'You mean Angelo wouldn't help? A pitiful wail came down the line. 'Oh, Terri, you've got to speak to him again. Beg him—anything! For my sake—and little Laura's!'

'Don't worry, I will.' She sounded a lot more confident than she felt. 'In the meantime, what I need from you are the names of some people on the island I can speak to who might be able to give me some clue. Friends, neighbours—anyone you can think of at all.'

After a few more unhappy sobs, Vicki reeled off a couple of names. 'They're our next-door neighbours on either side.' Then she added several more after a bit of prodding from Terri. 'Friends of Ruggero's from the Yacht Club. They might have some idea of where he's gone.'

Terri scribbled the names hastily on the little notepad that lay by the phone. 'I'll go and see them tomorrow,' she promised. 'And I'll call you back in a couple of days and let you know how I'm getting on. In the meantime, don't worry. One way or another, I'll get Laura back for you.'

'Oh, thank you, Terri. I know I can count on you.' Vicki blew her nose loudly down the phone, then enquired on a reciprocal note of concern, 'Are you sure you're all right staying at the Rosa? You'd be much more comfortable at the villa, you know.'

Terri had no doubt she would. The Rosa was far from being the Ritz. But all the same, she declined Vicki's offer with the same argument she had used in London. 'It wouldn't be very seemly for me to move into your house when Ruggero might come back at any time. Don't worry about me, I'm fine. Just you concentrate on keeping your spirits up.'

That had been three hours ago. Now, as Angelo's deadline ticked by, she lay on the narrow, stifling bed, the thin sheet tossed aside, and let the breeze from the shuttered window waft deliciously over her sticky flesh. Tomorrow, as promised, she would make a start. Armed with her evening-school Italian, she would tackle some of the names on her list and start tracking Laura down.

Yet something told her that was not where the solution lay. The solution lay with Angelo, up there in the Casa Grande. Hadn't Vicki once told her that not a leaf fell on the island without Angelo knowing about it? He was hiding something from her, she felt sure.

Restlessly, she turned over and stared into the night. So many mysteries. So many questions. And to all of them Angelo was the key. Eventually, she would have to face him again if she was to get to the bottom of it all.

In the meantime—she closed her eyes and smiled to

herself—she would quite enjoy being a thorn in his side.

Terri was up early next morning, and, after a breakfast of *cappuccino* and doughnuts at the *pensione*, the first thing she did was hire herself a car. 'For one week,' she told the man in the oily vest who handed over the keys. That should give her enough time.

After a quick study of the road map, she set out, following the narrow, twisting inland road, past hedges of prickly pears and almond and orange groves, skirting Falcon Mountain, to the west side of the island where Vicki and Ruggero's villa was. She would start with the neighbours first, she'd decided.

But a few sympathetic shrugs were all she got. A woman in a flowing turquoise caftan told her apologetically, 'Sorry, *signorina*. Not here.'

'*Dove?*' Terri persisted hopefully. 'Do you know where they've gone?'

But the woman just shrugged again. '*In vacanza, molto probabile.*' Then she spelled it out in English, in case the blonde stranger had failed to understand. 'On 'oliday, I think!'

Reluctant to leave empty-handed, Terri drove past Vicki's villa at least half a dozen times, praying for some sign that Ruggero and the baby had returned. She even peered through the windows, searching for some signs of life. But it was clear that there was no one at home.

By evening, she was no further forward. For one thing, she had been unable to track down half the people on her list, and the rest, though apparently willing, had been unable to help. Hot and exhausted, she decided to call it a day. After all, she had time. Tomorrow morning she would start again.

Lunch had been a hurried affair—so, partly out of hunger and partly to bolster her flagging spirits, she decided to treat herself to a slap-up dinner. She chose a little *trattoria* within walking distance of the *pensione* that had caught her eye in the course of her travels. Though tucked up a side street, according to the sign outside it boasted a garden at the back. Now that the temperature had dropped a bit, it would be pleasant to dine al fresco.

Most of the tables were already occupied when she arrived, and a hubbub of chatter and laughter filled the warm, scented air. If the waiter thought it odd to see a young foreign girl on her own, his expression gave nothing away. He escorted her to a quiet table at the back. '*Ecco, signorina,*' he smiled.

Terri ordered *spaghetti alla Strega* and a quarter carafe of wine and sat back to enjoy the animated spectacle of the couples and families who were gathered together, and the waiters weaving like acrobats between the crowded tables. She smiled contentedly to herself. This wasn't exactly a holiday, but it certainly beat the nine-to-five grind!

She was half-way through a swordfish cutlet when

suddenly she was uncomfortably conscious of a pair of lingering eyes directed at her from a nearby table. Cautiously, she half turned round, then abruptly turned away again as she found herself looking into a coarse, swarthy face, leering, hooded eyes, heavy lips contorted in a lewd, suggestive smile.

Annoyed, she kept her eyes fixed straight ahead, feeling her spine stiffen defensively, suddenly grateful that, quite unconsciously, she had taken Angelo's advice and was wearing a modest, round-necked cotton blouse and an equally modest long, loose skirt. In spite of what he had suggested, attentions of this sort were the last thing she'd been hoping to invite.

For the rest of the meal she studiedly kept her eyes averted, hoping that if she ignored him the man would simply tire of his unpleasant little game. But he was not so easily discouraged. She could still feel his gaze on her, like a grubby, disgusting paw. As the waiter brought a bowl of fruit, she asked for the bill. Her evening was spoiled. She just wanted to go.

She paid her bill and headed for the door, an angry resentment bubbling inside. How dared some sick-minded pervert spoil her evening like that? Then, on an impulse, she swung round on her way out to throw a look of condemnation at him. Let him realise the total contempt she felt! But her heart turned over uncomfortably in her breast as she saw that he was no longer there. The table where he had been sitting just a moment ago was empty now.

She left the bright lights of the *trattoria* with a faint squeeze of anxiety. It was a ten-minute walk through dimly lit streets back to the Pensione Rosa. Suddenly she was wishing, after all, that she hadn't ventured out alone.

But that was ridiculous, she chided herself as she marched briskly along the narrow pavement. The man had probably just finished his meal and left in perfect innocence. In spite of his earlier behaviour, there was no reason at all to believe that he was hiding up some alleyway in wait for her. It was just that melodramatic talk of Angelo's that had planted such silly fears in her head.

All the same, her heart very nearly stopped dead in her chest at a sudden movement at her back. She whirled round like a cat on hot coals, just in time to see a shadowy, dark figure dart into a doorway, out of sight. It was him—the man from the *trattoria*. She was absolutely sure of it.

Sheer panic gripped her as she started to run. 'Oh, God,' she prayed in sudden cold fear, 'please don't let him get me!'

But just then a jagged cobblestone caught the toe of her sandal and she lurched forward, stumbling helplessly. Her blood froze in her veins and her limbs turned to lead as a hand reached out from the shadows and grabbed her roughly by the arm.

CHAPTER THREE

SHE almost fell straight into his arms.

As the powerful grip that held her jerked her to her feet, a scream of sheer terror rose in her throat. Blindly she struggled, vainly trying to free herself from the band of steel around her arm. But, the more she struggled, the more cruelly the fingers tightened their grip.

She could feel the heat of his body pressing against hers, his breath on her cheek as he rasped at her, 'What the hell do you think you're doing?'

At the sound of the deep voice, her head snapped up and she found herself staring into a harsh, dark face, eyes as black as midnight, the wide mouth clamped in a hard, straight line. 'Dear heaven!' A wave of relief, spiked with anger, swept through her. 'What the devil do you think you're doing sneaking up on me like that?'

Angelo threw her a fierce look. 'What the devil do *you* think you're doing, wandering about the streets alone at this time of night?'

As he continued to hold her, she made another futile attempt to pull herself free. 'I wasn't wandering about the streets!' she spat. 'I was simply making my way back to the *pensione* after having dinner at a restaurant.' She eyed him resentfully. 'Is there some law against that?'

The black eyes narrowed impatiently. 'You fool! Do you think that was a sensible thing to do? As I've already pointed out to you, this isn't Hampstead Garden Suburb!'

Terri lowered her eyes. He was right, of course. But she wasn't about to admit that to him.

'And who was that man who was following you?' Angelo wanted to know.

Nor was she about to give him the satisfaction of knowing just how grateful she felt for his sudden appearance on the scene. She stared back defiantly at him. 'What man?' she bluffed.

A humourless smile curled round his lips. '*Cara mia*,' he intoned, 'either you are a liar, or an even bigger fool than I had taken you for. Your pursuer has gone now—while you and I were struggling—but allow me to give you some advice. If you insist on being so independent, then you must learn to be a little more vigilant.' Abruptly he released her, causing her to stagger back. 'You cannot always rely on someone like myself being on hand to bail you out of your scrapes.'

Terri rubbed her tingling arm. 'Don't worry,' she retorted, 'your services won't be required again!' From now on she would be doubly careful, if only just to keep him out of her hair! A sudden question occurred to her. 'What were you doing here, anyway?'

Although he had released her, he was still blocking her way, a tall, faintly threatening figure in a sand-coloured suit. Powerful, broad shoulders, lean hips, strong thighs, the muscular arms that were folded now across his chest possessing instant, hair-trigger reflexes, as she had already experienced for herself. Under the flickering sodium street-lights, the harsh lines of his forceful features seemed deeply scored in the dark-tanned face. He told her, 'I came for you.'

'For me?' The phrase had an ominous ring.

He smiled a grim smile. 'That is correct.' Then he went on to elaborate, 'However, be under no illusions. It was not for the pleasure of your company that I came to seek you out.'

She scowled back at him. That unlikely possibility had never even crossed her mind.

He continued, 'When I arrived at the Rosa looking for you, the *padrona* told me you had gone out. I waited a while and, when you didn't show, I decided to come and find you for myself.'

Terri frowned at him. Maybe that explained how he'd come to be so conveniently on hand, but it still didn't answer the question of why he'd come looking for her in the first place.

But, before she could put the question to him, he told her, 'However, I scarcely think we should be discussing private business in such a public place.' Without preamble, he took her arm and started to propel her along the narrow street. 'We shall be much more comfortable in my car.'

Terri started to protest, but decided to save her breath. Whatever Angelo had come to see her about, she might as well let him get it over with. Then perhaps he would be satisfied and, mercifully, let her go.

Just around the corner, a low red car was parked. The street where the Rosa was tucked away was only just wide enough to take one car. That, presumably, was why he'd parked here. As he pulled open the passenger door for her, she glanced at the black horse badge on the back. If nothing else, this would be a first. She had never ridden in a Ferrari before.

She sank into the soft leather upholstery and glanced across at him scathingly as he climbed in beside her. 'Isn't this a bit excessive just to go a couple of blocks?'

The big engine roared instantly to life. He flicked an amused glance back at her. 'Who said we were only going a couple of blocks?' he enquired wickedly.

'But the Rosa——'

'I know where the Rosa is. That's not where we're headed, *mia cara*.'

As the big car stole silently away from the kerb, Terri was suddenly aware of a nervous pulse throbbing in her throat. 'Where are you taking me?' she wanted to know.

Angelo did not gratify her with a reply. Instead, he said, 'I understand you have extended your booking at the Rosa for a further week.'

So he had been checking up on her. 'Do you have

any objections?' she shot back sarcastically.

'I'm afraid I do. I cannot allow it,' he informed her coolly.

'*Allow* it?' Terri stressed the word contemptuously.

But, before she could go any further, Angelo cut in, 'You are related to my family—however remote and tenuous the link. It is quite unthinkable that you should continue residence in such a place.'

'But the Rosa suits me very well. There's really no need for you to concern yourself.'

'Oh, but I do. While you are on Santa Pietrina, it is not seemly for you to stay in such a place. Your sister, after all, is a Montefalcone—however regrettable that fact may be.'

She threw him a shrewd look. So it was not her comfort that was his concern, merely the dignity of his family name. 'Well, I'm afraid I can't afford to move into the Mediterraneo,' she told him cuttingly, naming the island's four-star hotel. Nor would she allow him to pay for her to do so, if that was what he had in mind.

It seemed it was not. Even from her own sketchy knowledge of the island, Terri could tell that they were going in the wrong direction for that. Already they were starting to leave the clustered lights of the town behind, heading for the deserted inland road. A sudden irrational panic gripped her. Was she being kidnapped too?

Perhaps he could read what was in her mind, for he turned to reassure her with the hint of a smile, 'For the duration of your stay, one of the Casa Grande beach villas will be put at your disposal. I have already made arrangements for you to move in tonight.'

For a moment Terri was speechless. Surely that was jumping the gun a bit? 'What makes you think I want to move into one of the Casa Grande beach villas?' she shot at him indignantly.

He responded flatly, 'Whether you want to or not, that is the arrangement that has been made.'

'Is it?' Suddenly she was furious. His assumption was high-handed in the extreme. 'Well, I'm afraid I won't be able to move in tonight,' she told him. 'All my things are at the *pensione*. And there is also the small matter of settling the bill.'

'Wrong on both counts.' He smiled at her. 'Your luggage is in the back of the car. I had the *padrona* pack for you while I was waiting for you to arrive.' He raised one dark eyebrow in amusement. 'It's fortunate you don't have much stuff—the boot of this car is rather small.'

Why, the cheek of the man! 'You had no right to do that! And the bill?' She fumbled indignantly with her bag.

'Forget it.'

'I will not!' She made a quick calculation in her head and thrust a handful of notes at him. He probably spent more on toothpicks in a year, but it was the principle of the thing.

He stuffed the notes casually into the pocket of his jacket as he swung the car off the narrow road, through a wrought-iron gateway, already open, and on to a crunchy gravel-chip drive. 'We're here,' he told her—and suddenly, amid palm trees at the end of the drive, she could see an elegant, flat-roofed villa, its white walls adorned with sweet bougainvillaea.

As he drew to a halt and she climbed out, Terri caught the sharp tang of the sea. Then she spied, high on the cliff above them, the twinkling lights of the Casa Grande. So they had traversed the island from coast to coast and she had been dropped right into the falcon's back yard! She shivered slightly in the warm night air. It would have suited her much better to stay on where she was.

There were lights shining from the front, sea-facing side of the villa. Angelo lifted her bags from the boot of the Ferrari and led her, on long, brisk strides, up a short flight of stone steps and on to a wide, tiled terrace, then swiftly through the open french doors into the brightly lit room beyond.

Terri glanced round her. It was a cool, generously proportioned room, simply but elegantly furnished, with colourful dhurri rugs scattered across the marble-tiled floor. As Angelo laid down her bags, from the direction of what Terri guessed must be the kitchen a middle-aged man and woman appeared, both dressed in the familiar blue and black of the Montefalcone domestic retinue.

'Grazia and Salvatore,' Angelo informed her. 'They are here to look after you. Anything you require, I'm sure they'll be happy to see to it.' Then, in Italian, he introduced her to the couple. '*Questa è la nostra ospite, la Signorina Allan.'*

From her scant familiarity with the language, Terri was able to decipher the word for guest. As she nodded politely at the silent pair, she smiled a wry smile to herself. That was one way of putting it, she thought. Little were they to guess that she'd been press-ganged into coming here!

As Salvatore stepped forward to take charge of her bags, Angelo was already taking his leave. 'With the greatest reluctance, I must leave you now.' He bestowed a darkly ironic smile on her as he turned towards the door. 'I wish you *buonanotte*—and pleasant dreams.'

Then, almost before she had time to respond with a muttered 'Goodnight', he was heading out on to the terrace again and down the stone steps, out of sight, disappearing into the shadows like a thief in the night.

She stood and stared with a curious frown at the spot where he had been. Then, just a moment later, she heard the big car roar off down the drive.

That night Terri slept like a top. The air-conditioned villa was deliciously cool after the Rosa, the big, wide bed with its prettily embroidered sheets extravagantly comfortable. She woke just before nine o'clock, feeling thoroughly refreshed and in remarkably good spirits, considering the circumstances.

As she pushed open the shutters of her bedroom

window, she gasped in mingled surprise and delight. Down beyond the private gardens of the villa, bright with huge, semi-tropical blooms, stretched a vast, gently moving mass of the deepest cerulean blue. The villa was right on the edge of the sea. Terri smiled to herself. It was paradise.

Or it would have been, she reminded herself, were it not for the sinister, dark presence she could feel, even now, breathing down her neck. She glanced towards the high cliff-top. He was up there, watching her. It was undoubtedly, as much as anything, in order to keep an eye on her that he had brought her here.

Grazia had breakfast waiting for her out on the terrace. Fruit juice, oven-fresh *brioches* and a huge, fragrant pot of *caffellatte*. It was just as she was helping herself to her second cup that Terri spied out of the corner of her eye her little rented Autobianchi car parked in the shade under some trees. Someone from the Casa Grande had brought it round earlier, Grazia explained to her when she enquired. Inwardly, Terri made a face. The hand of Angelo de Montefalcone was everywhere, it seemed.

Her first task after breakfast was to give Vicki a ring. 'Just to let you know I've moved,' she explained after divulging her new address.

Vicki sounded pleased at the news. 'Do you think that means that Angelo's relenting?'

Quite the contrary, to Terri's mind, though she kept her opinion to herself. Instead, she soothed,

'Who knows? I'll keep working on him anyway.'

'Thanks, Terri. I'm really grateful,' Vicki assured her. Then she added as Terri was about to hang up, 'When you find Ruggero, tell him I'm sorry—and that I love him very much.'

Terri laid the phone down thoughtfully. 'Tell him I'm sorry.' So, Vicki regretted their little row. It was beginning to sound as though not only did she want her baby back, but she was having a change of heart about her marriage as well. Even better, Terri decided. All the more reason to track Ruggero down.

The couple of phone calls she made next—to names on Vicki's list—unfortunately both drew blanks. 'Try later,' she was advised. 'Maybe after lunch.'

She glanced outside at the bright, sunny sky and decided to give herself the morning off. Then she hurriedly changed into her bikini and announced to Grazia that she was going down to the beach.

The beach was pleasantly secluded, fringed with lazily waving palms. And, miraculously, there wasn't another soul in sight. This stretch must be private, she decided, arranging her towel over one of the sunbeds and dumping the rest of her things in the shade of the big red sun umbrella.

A small fishing-boat had been drawn up at the water's edge, a short distance away, its hull creaking softly in the gently lapping tide. A soothing sound,

Terri decided as she stretched out on the sunbed, taking advantage of the privacy to slip off her bikini-top and expose her small, rose-tipped breasts to the sun.

She closed her eyes and let her thoughts drift pleasantly away. This was the first real opportunity to relax she'd had since her arrival on Santa Pietrina. For a couple of hours, at least, she would consign her problems to the back of her mind.

Of course, she ought to have known better. She had just finished toasting her back and had rolled over to expose her front again, lazily smoothing a top-up of tanning lotion over her sun-warmed flesh, when all at once a shadow fell over her.

'Would you like me to help you with that?' a deep voice enquired.

Terri blinked and sat up with a start, her hands flying to her naked breasts. She glared at him, her cheeks crimson with embarrassment. 'What are you doing here?' she spat.

Angelo was wearing a loose white shirt, the sleeves rolled up casually to his elbows, and a pair of white cotton trousers folded up around his ankles. Against the crisp white cloth his skin looked very dark, the thick collar-length hair as black and glossy as a raven's wing. He didn't answer her question. Instead, almost coarsely, he remarked, 'Why don't you remove your bottom half as well, and give your audience their money's worth?'

Already Terri was fumbling for her bikini-top, acutely conscious of his eyes on her. She glanced self-consciously around. 'What audience?' she demanded. 'There's no one here.'

'Oh, no?' Angelo raised a dark eyebrow at her. 'I seem to recall that's what you said last night.' Then he continued, as he lowered his tall frame on to a neighbouring sunbed less than an arm's span away, 'Perhaps in the more blasé tourist resorts to which you are accustomed, such immodest practices are accepted as part of the scenery. In this more backward part of the world, a half-naked woman lying on the beach is guaranteed to attract curious eyes.'

Lest she doubt the truth of his words, he slipped one hand into the pocket of his trousers and drew out a handful of coins. Then, ensuring that he had her full attention, he tossed them in the direction of the fishing-boat. A moment later two dark, tousled heads appeared and a couple of grinning urchins came darting out from behind the hull to scoop up the coins from the sand. Then, squealing with laughter, they turned and went scampering off across the beach.

Terri cursed herself, feeling a fool. Little had she suspected that she was providing a peep-show for the local youth! 'I thought I was alone,' she protested.

'As I have told you before, you must learn to be a little more vigilant,' Angelo observed. Then he added in an amused tone as a figure appeared from behind a palm tree, carrying a tray of drinks, 'At least you have spared Salvatore's blushes. I'm sure he would not have approved at all.'

As the man set the tray down on a tiny trestle-table, then silently took his leave again, Angelo told her. 'Grazia told me you were here when I called at the villa. I thought you might be ready for a drink.'

He handed her a tall glass of freshly squeezed *limonata* in crushed ice and suggested, 'Perhaps we ought to move to the shade. For someone of your colouring, it is not wise to stay too long in the sun.'

He was right. Already she was starting to feel a warning glow. Disdaining his assistance, Terri pulled her sunbed back into the shade of the sun umbrella and eyed him as she took a mouthful of her drink. It seemed, to her intense displeasure, as he drew his own sunbed alongside, that he was not in any particular hurry to go. As though reading her thoughts, he said without smiling, 'I expect you're wondering what I'm doing here.'

'As a matter of fact, I wasn't,' she retorted, not smiling either. She'd decided the moment she had set eyes on him that he'd come to put more pressure on her to go.

'But I shall tell you anyway.' He regarded her over the top of his glass, the dark eyes narrowing as they scanned her face. 'I hear you've been speaking to my cousin's neighbours and some of his friends from the Yacht Club.'

Terri frowned wryly to herself. What was it Vicki had said? Not a leaf falls . . . How right she had been!

'I simply asked if they knew where Ruggero was,' she defended now. 'I didn't tell them why I was asking. I was quite discreet.'

'Alas, not quite discreet enough. The news got straight back to me.' He gave her a long look. 'I have already warned you, *mia cara*. One warning was evidently not enough.'

With difficulty, Terri held his eyes. 'If you would just tell me where your cousin is, I wouldn't need to be indiscreet.'

He lowered his gaze and laid his glass in the sand. 'I've told you, I don't know where Ruggero is.'

She felt irritated by the bare-faced lie. In a scathing tone, she pointed out, 'Considering he works for you, you seem remarkably unconcerned about his sudden disappearance.'

Angelo ran one thoughtful finger down the strong, straight bridge of his nose. 'Take my word for it, Montefalcone Navigation will not grind to a halt in his absence.' He smiled an amused, sardonic smile. 'If that is what is on your mind, you really have no cause for concern.'

Terri flung a harsh look back at him. 'That's nice to know.' Montefalcone Navigation, like everything else in this man's world, would be directed and controlled exclusively by him. He would not rely on others. The reins of power would be firmly in his hands. She straightened, flicking back her long blonde hair, and challenged him, 'But what about Laura? You may not care about Ruggero, but what about his little daughter? Don't you care what's happened to her?'

Angelo gave her a straight look. 'I thought we had already established that my cousin is an excellent father. A considerably better father than your sister is a mother. There is no doubt in my mind that the child is best left where she is.'

'I don't agree.'

'Then we must agree to differ. The fact remains that I am unable to help you. You would do well to return as soon as possible to England and waste no more time here.' He paused, then added in a more persuasive tone, 'I'm sure you must have some sweetheart there who is waiting for you.'

Terri gave him a glacial look. 'I can't see what business it is of yours—but, as a matter of fact, I don't.'

He looked surprised. 'Surely, now that you no longer have a fiancé to hold you back, you have several young men in tow?'

She knew from the twist in his voice that he was deliberately insulting her, exactly as he had been doing right from the very start. And suddenly she'd had enough of it. It was time to set the record straight.

She took a deep breath. 'I don't have to explain anything about myself to you, but I resent your constant allusions. I do not have several young men in my life. I never have. If you really want to know, the only man who has ever merited a mention in my life is my ex-fiancé, Steve.' Steadily, the blue eyes met the black. Before he could interrupt, she hurried on, 'I met him four years ago, just after he graduated from college.' She could have added that she had never intended the relationship to get serious, but instead she continued, 'Shortly after we started going out together, he was in a road accident in which his younger brother was killed. Steve was driving. They said the accident was his fault. He was blamed for the death of his brother.'

She took a deep breath, remembering that terrible time and all the traumas that were to follow. 'Steve was devastated. He fell apart.' Wasn't that why she had stayed with him, supporting him and pulling him through the bad times when even his family turned against him? She spared her audience the sordid details of how he had turned to drink, allowed his career to founder and at one point attempted suicide. But she could tell she had Angelo's full attention. The dark eyes were narrowed, the jaw set in a firm, hard line.

'Eventually he began to recover, and by then the two of us had grown quite close. He asked me to marry him. I agreed.' She omitted the painful heartsearching that had preceded her decision. Their relationship, after all, had always been chaste—more a friendship than a love-affair—but perhaps in time it would develop, she had thought, and besides, it was her duty to stick with him. Steve's recovery at that point had been so fragile. If she had stepped aside, he might easily have fallen apart again.

She had been staring down at the sand, feeling her

heart thud in her chest as she relived the painful memories. Now she raised her eyes to meet Angelo's, oddly aware of the still, quiet strength that seemed to flow out to her from him. In a low voice, he told her, 'You don't have to tell me this, you know.'

'I want to.' And, for some reason, she did. She bit her lip and continued, 'Our wedding was set for last September. We'd found a house, everything. Then, on my birthday last May, I received a letter through the post.' She smiled a wry smile. 'It was from Steve. He'd changed his mind. He told me he was about to marry some girl he'd been seeing secretly for a couple of months. And that was the end of that. I never heard from him again.'

She dropped her gaze once more to the sand. How to explain that it wasn't her heart that had been broken? She had never really been in love with Steve. It was the callous betrayal that had hurt. After all the years of standing by him, he hadn't even had the decency to meet her face to face. Just a six-line letter through the post without a word of apology or regret. Her belief in the human race had died a little that day.

Since then, there had been no man in Terri's life. And, as though in reaction against all the wasted time, a kind of restlessness had overtaken her. She had given up her permanent job and taken to temporary work. The constant challenge of change helped to keep her mind occupied. She looked across at Angelo. 'So you see, my private life is far from being the frivolous, fun-filled merry-go-round that you seem to think it is.'

For a long moment he said nothing, just continued to stare at her with those deeply penetrating black eyes. 'So,' he said at last, 'you spent three years of your life looking after a man who was not worth the sand on your feet—and now you are repeating the folly with your equally undeserving sister.'

His reaction shocked her. There was no shred of sympathy, just harsh hostility in his voice.

'What is it, Teresa— do you enjoy being used by other people?'

A strange emotion shot through Terri, along with the indignation she felt. It was the first time for years that anyone had called her Teresa. Illogically, she felt herself flush. Floundering, she looked away. 'Vicki's my sister,' she defended weakly. 'I've always looked after her.'

'Then it's time you stopped.' Angelo got to his feet. 'Start looking out for yourself for a change.'

And he would be the perfect one to teach her that selfish philosophy! The supremely self-sufficient Angelo de Montefalcone. The ultimate egotist! Suddenly shaky with anger and frustration, Terri started to clamber to her feet—and awkwardly knocked against the little trestle-table where the drinks were laid. Stumbling, she swung round in an effort to save them, and might have made it had not

Angelo caught her by the arm.

'Let them fall,' he admonished her, as the tray, along with the glasses, slid with a dull thump to the sand. 'The fate of such small things is of no account.'

His fingers were like fire around her wrist as he snatched her round to look at him, and the sudden proximity of his long, lean frame was deeply, alarmingly threatening. She held her breath as he pulled her closer, feeling the loose cotton of his shirt brush wantonly against her half-naked breasts, fiercely, almost agonisingly aware of the hard male thighs that were pressed against her own.

His face was inches away, the wide, sensuously carved lips within a hair's breadth of brushing against her brow. Through thick black lashes he looked down at her, the dark eyes burning with a raw, devouring fire.

The falcon, Terri thought in sudden wild panic. And I am his prey.

Then, as she started to struggle, he released his grip and all the intensity of a moment before seemed to drop away from him. Calmly he told her, 'In life, one must learn to distinguish between those causes that are worthy of our efforts and those that are not.' He paused before adding, 'And your dear sister, alas, falls most assuredly into the latter category.'

She stared at him. 'You're wrong, you know.'

He shook his head. 'I wish I were, but I'm not.' Then he continued unwaveringly to hold her eyes as he reached into the back pocket of his trousers and produced a folded envelope. He held it out to her. 'In there you will find a first-class air ticket back to London, plus a voucher for a two weeks' stopover at a top hotel in Brindisi. I think that should more than compensate for all the pointless trouble you've put yourself to.'

A cold, raw resentment flooded through Terri. So he was adding bribery to coercion now! Without a word, she raised the envelope and, very deliberately, ripped it in two. Then in two again . . . and again . . . till it was reduced to confetti in her hands. Then, in an extravagantly contemptuous gesture, she flung the ripped pieces into the air and watched with a thin smile of satisfaction as they fluttered in a snowstorm to the sand.

Angelo eyed her, his expression dark. 'You may live to regret that, *mia cara*,' he said. And, without a backward glance, he turned and strode off across the sand.

CHAPTER FOUR

OUT of sheer frustrated anger and spite, as soon as Angelo had gone, Terri went straight back to the villa and got to work on Vicki's list again.

The first two phone calls drew a blank. Either Ruggero's friends were lying to protect him, or they really were under the illusion that he had simply gone off on holiday somewhere with his wife and child. The third number was one she had already tried a couple of times before, but there had always either been no answer or it had been engaged. It was the home number of Enzo Tardelli—according to what Vicki had said, Ruggero's special friend at the Yacht Club. Surely, if anyone knew Ruggero's whereabouts, it would be Enzo?

To her delight, this time a female voice answered. '*Pronto?*'

'*Pronto,*' Terri replied. '*Per favore, c'è il Signor Enzo Tardelli?*' Is Mr Enzo Tardelli there?

The woman, picking up Terri's English accent, answered helpfully in perfect English. 'No, I'm sorry, he's away on business this week. Perhaps I can help you or take a message? I'm Signora Tardelli, his wife.'

Terri thought quickly. 'I think I really need to talk

to your husband. It's an important matter regarding Ruggero Montefalcone. I'm Vicki's sister, Terri,' she explained.

'Ah . . .' There was a short pause at the other end, then the woman told her, 'In that case, you'll have your chance to speak to him on Saturday night. At the party.'

'Party?'

'Angelo's party at the Casa Grande. Enzo will definitely be back for that.'

Terri smiled to herself. 'Good,' she told the woman politely. 'I'll look out for him there.' And she felt her smile broaden as she laid down the phone. So Angelo was throwing a party. That was indeed interesting news. For no doubt everyone who was anyone on the island would be there—including all the people who might be able to help her in her search.

Inwardly she hugged herself as the plan in her head began to take shape. On Saturday Angelo was going to have one extra, uninvited guest.

On Saturday night, just after nine, Terri climbed into the little white Autobianchi and set off nervously for the Casa Grande. Gatecrashing private parties was not something she had a great deal of experience at, but this evening could provide her with opportunities far too valuable to miss. In spite of her tremors, she told herself, it would be well worth risking Angelo's wrath.

With Grazia's assistance, she had worked her

shoulder-length blonde tresses into a stylish plait down the back of her head, the end secured with a simple gilt bow. The style lent an air of sophistication to the simple outfit she was wearing—a blue and white floral-printed two-piece with a full, floaty skirt and crossover top.

She smiled wryly to herself as she made her way along the cliff road. Even if she had had the foresight to bring something a little more dressy with her, she doubted it would have fitted the bill. Her well-planned but modest wardrobe back home boasted nothing that would come even close to the *haute couture* elegance she expected to see in evidence tonight. Angelo's little party, she suspected, would be like nothing she had ever experienced before.

There was only one problem: how to get in. Terri had never entered the Casa Grande through the main gates before and, in spite of Grazia's directions, she was having some difficulty finding her way—until she spied a trio of limousines in convoy just ahead and decided to tag along behind. Her suspicion that they contained party guests was almost instantly confirmed as they swept round the perimeter of the old fortress walls, then through high, turreted portals into a courtyard where a fountain played.

She parked the little car in an inconspicuous corner and climbed out, feeling slightly overwhelmed by the sights and sounds that met her eyes and ears. The huge carved doors of the Casa Grande stood open and, spilling out into the night from the brightly lit, sumptuous interior came the sounds of music and movement and laughter. The party was evidently in full swing.

Desperately trying to conceal her nerves, she attached herself to the group of guests whose arrival had so conveniently coincided with her own, and allowed herself to be ushered inside by a young man in a blue and black uniform who took the women's wraps and stoles. Then she was following them across a mirrored hallway, along an elegant corridor and into an enormous room already thronged with glittering guests.

Just for a moment she had to pause and fight back the alarm that had risen in her throat. Angelo's guests were all so grand. The women blazed with expensive jewels as they stood around in their silks and tulles, while their dinner-jacketed companions bore that faintly daunting look of men well-accustomed to signing cheques with a formidable row of zeros on the end.

As the little group she had sneaked in with quickly dispersed among the crowd to cries of welcome from their friends, Terri was suddenly left feeling stranded, hotly self-conscious, painfully awkward, as though she had strayed into some alien world. In a surge of panic it crossed her mind that maybe she should just turn and leave before anyone noticed she was there.

But already it was too late for that. A waiter appeared soundlessly at her side. 'What would the *signorina* like to drink?'

She hesitated.

'Champagne?'

She nodded. 'Yes, please.' What could be more fitting, in such a setting, than champagne?

As if by magic, another waiter with a tray of fizzing champagne flutes appeared before her. 'Please, *signorina*,' he invited.

Terri helped herself. '*Grazie*.' And she took a bubbling mouthful as both waiters melted inconspicuously back into the crowd.

Over the rim of her glass she eyed the sea of unknown faces. There was no sign of Angelo. At least that was something to be grateful for. Perhaps she could manage to infiltrate his guests and get the information she needed without him even realising she was there. She frowned as she glanced round. But where to begin?

It was just then that she was aware of a pair of eyes on her. A dark-haired girl in an ivory-coloured dress that had probably cost almost as much as Terri paid annually in rent was watching her from a nearby group. Openly assessing and dismissive at the same time, the girl's eyes travelled over her, taking in the chain-store two-piece, the wrists and fingers naked of jewellery, the cheap, unadorned shoes. And, without even opening her mouth, she managed quite eloquently to say, 'What the hell are *you* doing here?'

Bitch! Summoning all her poise, Terri straightened and glared back at her. Then, with a deliberate toss of her head, she started to turn away—and collided straight into another waiter who had materialised before her bearing a tray of colourful hors-d'oeuvre.

'Excuse me, *signorina*.' The waiter was apologetic as, with an expert flick of the wrist, he twisted the tray deftly out of harm's way. But Terri's reflexes were not quite so instantaneous, nor so well-trained. She cursed inwardly, feeling the colour rise to her cheeks, as the contents of the champagne glass went flying indecorously over her arm. She did not have to look up to see the look of malicious amusement on the dark-haired girl's face.

'Allow me. I'll deal with this.'

All at once a strong, tanned masculine hand reached out to relieve her of her empty glass, then impatiently waved the waiter away as he arrived with a fresh flute of champagne. 'That won't be necessary,' the deep voice said. 'I don't think the young lady will be staying.'

Still flushed with embarrassment, Terri looked up to find Angelo standing right beside her—and was totally unprepared for the way her heart stirred at the sight of him. He was dressed in an immaculate white jacket, black trousers, white silk shirt and black bow-tie. The dark hair gleamed beneath the overhead lights. The piercing black eyes seemed to hypnotise.

But the expression in them was hard, his tone sarcastic as he told her, 'I don't remember requesting the pleasure of your company here tonight.'

'You didn't.' Terri was struggling to regain her

cool. 'But I assumed that was simply an oversight and decided to come along anyway.'

His lips curled in a smile, but without amusement. 'You assumed wrongly, *mia cara*. The omission was no oversight. The reason I did not invite you was that I did not want you here.' He held her eyes with ruthless candour. 'You see, I know very well what it is you're after . . .' He paused, the dark gaze scanning her face. 'And since I have no intention of allowing you to pester my guests with your futile interrogations, permit me to accompany you back to your car.'

Defiantly, Terri straightened her shoulders and took a step back, away from him. 'I had no idea that Sicilian aristocrats were quite so inhospitable,' she said.

'And if I had not already had the displeasure of knowing your sister, I might have said I had no idea that supposedly well brought up young English girls had so little idea of how to behave. As it is, I know all too well.' The steely dark eyes fastened with hers. 'I repeat, kindly permit me to accompany you back to your car.'

Already one impatient hand was reaching out to cup her elbow, discreetly, yet inexorably, propelling her towards the door. Terri felt herself stiffen in response, uncertain what her next move should be. Then, in a sudden flash of inspiration, she jerked her arm free and swung round on him. 'If you lay one hand on me again, I warn you, I'll make the most terrible scene!'

For one split second, he hesitated, and she knew she had touched his Achilles' heel. An ugly scene would be the last thing he would want disrupting his elegant soirée. The black eyes narrowed. '*Maladetta troia*! You're even worse than your shameless sister!' The strong, tanned hand hovered hesitantly, not quite certain of her threat.

As they stood there, poised, glaring at one another like a couple of bad-tempered dogs, Terri's heart was pounding in her breast. All at once she was no more certain than he that she had the guts to carry out her threat.

Fortunately she was not put to the test. At that moment, a refined English voice made a timely interruption. 'Angelo, there you are! We haven't had a chance to tell you how much we're enjoying your lovely party!'

As one, the dark-haired man and the slim blonde girl turned to find at their elbow, smiling unsuspectingly at them, a distinguished-looking grey-haired gentleman and his slightly younger, attractive wife. Angelo recovered his composure instantly. 'Peter. Susan.' He deferred to them with a slight inclination of his head. 'I'm so glad you could come.' Then, with a reluctance that possibly only Terri sensed, he turned to her. 'Allow me to introduce you to Teresa—Vicki's sister. Teresa, meet Peter and Susan Donaldson, the island's longest-standing British residents.'

It was the first time in Terri's hearing that he had managed to pronounce her sister's name without even the hint of a sneer in his voice. Oddly, she felt grateful to him for that.

The couple shook hands with her warmly. 'Vicki's sister, are you?' Susan smiled. 'I would never have guessed it to look at you. You're not a bit like her, you know.'

Terri shook her head, carefully avoiding Angelo's eyes, yet almost tangibly aware of the cynical smile that had crept over his face. 'No,' she agreed. 'Most people say we're quite different.'

'But I thought Vicki and Ruggero had gone off on hol——?'

As Peter left the question dangling in the air, his expression apologising for his indiscretion, Terri remained deliberately silent, leaving the task of explaining this apparent irregularity to her reluctant host. Let's hear you talk your way out of this one! she thought maliciously to herself.

She need not have worried. 'Teresa had some private business on the island.' Smoothly, Angelo took charge. 'It may appear an unfortunate piece of mistiming that she should arrive here at a time when her sister and Ruggero are away, but——' he shrugged broad shoulders and turned to Terri with a totally convincing smile '—it simply means that I have all to myself the pleasure of looking after her.'

As the black eyes locked with the blue, Terri couldn't suppress a smile—and a sneaking, unwilling admiration for the total composure of the man. An unwilling admiration, too, for the effortless aura of control he exuded over all that surrounded him. The eye of the hurricane, she thought. Nothing would ever throw him.

As a waiter hovered near them with a tray of drinks, Terri helped herself to a flute of champagne. Try and throw me out now! her eyes challenged him as she raised the glass to her lips and drank.

But his attention had been momentarily diverted. From the far side of the room a stunning redhead in a glossy green dress was waving animatedly across at him. With a smile and a nod, he acknowledged the girl's waves, then threw a quick, apologetic glance at the Donaldsons and a more lingering look of warning at Terri. 'Excuse me for a moment, please. I see that some more guests have arrived.'

Sighing silently with relief, Terri watched as he moved off into the crowd, then observed with a wry smile as he was greeted with enthusiastic kisses, first by the girl in green, then by another one in red. As Susan followed her eyes, and her train of thought, exclaiming with an almost girlish giggle, 'Angelo's a very popular man!', Terri suddenly found herself remembering Vicki's remark about his weakness for good-looking women.

'Quite so.' Though, now that she knew him better herself, she was aware of the over-simplicity of her sister's statement. Angelo was undoubtedly a ladies' man. He had the looks, the charm, the charisma, the poise. And there was a sensuality in those deep, dark eyes that suggested he might even have a tendency at times to over-indulge himself with the opposite sex.

But a weakness? Never. Somehow, when proposed in association with Angelo, the very word had a hollow ring.

She turned her attention back to the Donaldsons, anxious to take advantage of her new-found liberty. She made a show of looking round the room, then enquired in a casual voice, 'I was looking for Enzo Tardelli and his wife. I don't suppose you've seen them, have you?'

Peter frowned and looked around. 'I was speaking to Enzo earlier.' Then Susan chipped in, 'Look, there they are! Over there by the balcony doors.' She pointed in the direction of a tall man with a moustache and a slim, fair-haired woman in a peacock-blue dress who were standing on the edge of a larger group.

Terri stole a quick glance over her shoulder to check that Angelo was still otherwise engaged, then, with a polite smile, she excused herself. 'Forgive me, but I promised to have a word with them.' There was no point in wasting time questioning the Donaldsons. They, quite evidently, could tell her nothing.

'You go ahead, dear,' Susan smiled. 'It's been lovely meeting you.'

'You too.' With a final polite nod, Terri detached herself. Then, head down, keeping her movements inconspicuous, she headed for the balcony doors and paused at the side of the fair-haired woman. 'Signora Tardelli?' she enquired.

The woman turned with a polite smile to look at

her. '*Si*,' she confirmed.

'I'm Terri, Vicki's sister. Remember, we spoke on the phone the other day?'

'Of course!' The polite smile warmed. 'You said you wanted to speak to my husband.' She nodded in the direction of the tall, moustached man. 'Well, here he is.'

Now Enzo addressed her. '*Si, signorina*. How can I help?'

Carefully, Terri cleared her throat and snatched another quick glance across her shoulder. 'It's Ruggero I want to talk to you about. I understand you're a good friend of his.'

Enzo Tardelli smiled. 'I like to think so,' he replied. 'In fact, I like to think I'm good friends with all the Montefalcone family.'

Damn! In that case, she must phrase her question with a measure of diplomacy. She fumbled mentally for a moment, then put to him, 'I need to get in touch with Ruggero rather urgently, but . . .' She shrugged in mock embarrassment. 'I know that he's gone away—and I know this must sound silly—but I don't know where he's gone.'

Enzo frowned. 'I don't know for definite either. I seem to remember his mentioning a business trip to Germany some time this month. I sort of assumed that he'd gone there.'

As Signora Tardelli frowned, 'How very naughty of Vicki to disappear without telling you where she was going!' Terri fought back the urge to tell her that she knew all too well where Vicki was, and that her sister was no wiser than herself as to her husband's whereabouts.

Instead she enquired, 'Germany, you say. Whereabouts in Germany?'

Enzo paused. 'I think he said Germany—in which case, almost certainly Hamburg. But it could have been Rotterdam. He often goes to the Netherlands too.'

Suddenly Terri's brain was buzzing. This was her biggest breakthrough yet. She was only half listening as the Signora put to her, 'It's nice that Vicki managed to get away with him this time, just as she always used to do before little Laura was born—but rather inconvenient for you if you were expecting to find them here.'

Then Enzo suggested, 'But why not just ask Angelo? He's bound to know where Ruggero is.'

Terri made a wry face to herself, but was forestalled in the accompanying wry remark she was about to make as Enzo's face suddenly broke into a smile.

'Talk of the devil!' he exclaimed.

Talk of the devil, indeed! All at once, a firm hand was on her arm and her champagne glass removed from her grasp as a deep voice said, 'Forgive me for interrupting, but I believe this is our dance.'

Terri turned, feeling her heart give an anxious lurch as she looked up into glittering black eyes. As he glanced at her companions—'I hope you will excuse us'—the hand tightened on her arm, almost making her wince. This wasn't so much an invitation to dance as a forcible physical abduction!

And there was little point in resisting it. Effortlessly, and still with that composed smile on his face, Angelo was drawing her away. Then a hard hand in the small of her back was propelling her without ceremony out on to an enormous balcony where an orchestra played and couples danced.

Like a rag doll he jerked her round to face him and pulled her roughly into his arms, one hand hard and restraining at her back, the other locking hers in a vice-like grip. 'You refuse to be warned, *mia cara*,' he ground. 'I thought I told you to leave my guests alone.'

She felt like a prisoner in his arms as he steered her into the centre of the floor. She glared at him with hostile blue eyes. 'You have no one to blame but yourself if I end up having to pester your guests. All you had to do was tell me yourself where Ruggero had gone.' Then she couldn't resist adding on a note of triumph, 'But I don't need your help any more. Enzo Tardelli told me all I need to know.'

One dark eyebrow lifted at her. 'Oh? And what did Enzo tell you?' he asked.

There was no reason to keep what she had learned from him. On the contrary, perhaps she could judge from Angelo's reaction whether what Enzo had told her was accurate or not. She said, watching him closely, 'He told me he's gone to Hamburg—or, possibly, to Rotterdam.'

But Angelo's expression gave nothing away. He

smiled a thinly humourless smile. 'In that case, can we look forward to your imminent departure for northern Europe?'

'Perhaps.' She decided to play along with him, for there were in fact a couple of things she still needed to know. She forced herself to smile sweetly. 'You must know the names of the people he deals with in these places, which hotels he stays in, that sort of thing. Just give me a couple of phone numbers and a couple of addresses—then, I promise, I'll be on my way.'

Equally sweetly, he smiled back. 'And why should I do that?' he asked.

'You said you wanted to get rid of me.'

'I also said, if you will recall, that I have no intention whatsoever of assisting you in your little mission. I thought I had made that perfectly clear.'

'Wouldn't it be worth co-operating this once just to get me out of your hair?'

He held her eyes and smiled a harsh smile as he spun her smoothly across the floor. 'I have numerous ways of dealing with people who get in my hair, *mia cara*. Co-operation is not one of them.'

Terri was aware of a shiver down her spine as she looked up into those midnight eyes—so deep, so dark, so uncompromising. And suddenly, too, she was acutely conscious of the overwhelming raw male closeness of him. The pressure of his broad chest against her breasts, the strong hand at her waist, the rhythmic, fleeting brush of his thighs.

Yet, she told herself firmly, as her pulse began to quicken, he held her like a captor, not a seducer. That the intimacy of his nearness should feel so cruelly seductive was a foolish and wholly irrational reaction—and one that was faintly alarming somehow.

As she tried, unsuccessfully, to move away, he enquired, his tone casual once more, 'So what other little gems of information have you managed to uncover over the past couple of days?'

'None.' She lowered her eyes, avoiding the dark gaze on her face. 'Everyone I've spoken to seems to be conveniently under the illusion that Vicki and Ruggero are on holiday.'

'That is convenient.'

As he smiled, she glanced up again and found her eyes following the curve of his mouth. Hastily she tore them away. 'I would say you have them all very well-trained. Even if they knew anything, I very much doubt they'd say.'

A gleam of amusement shone in his eyes. 'Yes, they are extremely loyal, I'm happy to say. Though, contrary to your suggestion, I take no credit for the fact.'

Terri eyed him. 'How modest! But a little difficult to believe. It's my impression that you have this whole damned island—and everyone on it—all neatly tied up, in your control.' As he simply smiled, denying nothing, she goaded, 'And I'll bet I know how you do it, too. A little bit of bullying here, a little bit of pressure there.'

To her annoyance, Angelo continued to look amused. 'One must apply whatever methods are effective, *mia cara*.'

'And you're the type of man who'll stop at nothing in order to get your way.' She narrowed her eyes disapprovingly at him, hating the way he was laughing at her. 'Tell me,' she added recklessly, 'are you as coldly calculating in all other areas of your life?'

There was a sudden subtle change in the tenor of his smile. The hand on her waist seemed to shift just a fraction. Deliberately he held her eyes. 'Which areas of my life specifically, Teresa?'

She looked away. 'Others, generally,' she answered awkwardly. Her original question had been rhetorical, and she was wishing now that she had kept it to herself.

'By general, you mean personal, I take it?'

What a clumsy fool she had been! Her stomach clenched as she protested, 'I didn't mean anything in particular.'

'Ah, but I think you did—and, since it interests you so much, allow me the privilege of answering you.' He paused, his eyes on her face, thoroughly enjoying watching her squirm. 'What was the question again? Am I as coldly calculating in my personal relationships as I appear to be in other areas of my life?'

As he paused again, Terri cut in, 'You don't have to answer. I don't really want to know.'

But he was simply taking pleasure in lingering over his reply. He smiled wickedly at her. 'No, Teresa,' he confessed. 'In the more intimate areas of my life, cold is an adjective that has never been applied to me.'

In spite of herself, she felt her face flame. 'I've already told you I don't want to know.'

However, Angelo wasn't through with embarrassing her yet. 'But don't just take my word for it, *cara*. Should you wish to ascertain for yourself by indulging in a bit of market research, I'm sure that could easily be arranged.'

Boldly, the black eyes swept her face and, abruptly, Terri dropped her gaze as a spark flared inside her in hot response to the deep, elemental, overtly sexual message that had passed between them then. All at once, Angelo's physical closeness seemed more than seductive. Suddenly it was threatening. Bristling with danger—and a sharp, sweet sense of promise.

For the remainder of the dance she did her best to concentrate on the music, desperately struggling to distance herself, at least mentally, from him. Then suddenly the music stopped, and with a kind of anguished relief she felt his hand drop from her waist and breathed again as the gap between their two bodies widened and he took a step back away from her. Now he would escort her back to the edge of the dance-floor and she could gather herself once more.

Not so. At the very moment of her release a man in a head waiter's uniform stepped out on to the balcony and announced to the assembled company that the buffet was served. As a murmur of approval went round the guests, Angelo's fingers closed round her arm and she felt her heart sink as she heard him say, 'Perhaps you would do me the honour of joining me for dinner?' Almost imperceptibly, his fingers tightened their grip. 'I think I would feel happier if I could continue to keep an eye on you.'

Next minute he was steering her across the balcony to where a line of laden trestle-tables had been arranged. 'Smile, *cara*,' he instructed her, his hand on her waist. 'Try to look as though you're enjoying this.'

The irony of her situation was that there were plenty who would have loved to have been in her place. Over the platters of risotto and lobster and fresh salad, she was aware of more than one pair of disappointed female eyes boring into her back. The privilege of partnering their handsome, highly eligible host for dinner was evidently considered to be something of a prize.

She glanced up over a dish of dressed crab to catch the dark-haired girl in the ivory-coloured dress eyeing her with unrestrained dislike. And in spite of the utter falseness of her own position Terri took pleasure in summoning up a coyly triumphant little smile. That's what you get for being such a snob! she thought.

As she and Angelo settled themselves at one of the little tables overlooking the bay, they were joined by another couple—Gianna and Leonardo, a glamorous local lady solicitor and her amusing, articulate accountant husband. As the conversation switched gear and took on a more general, less personal tone, somewhat to her own surprise Terri found herself settling back and thoroughly enjoying herself. Their companions were lively, refreshingly unstuffy company, and Angelo, she was discovering, besides being an immaculately attentive escort—no one would ever have guessed it was all a front—was a witty and perceptive story-teller.

Beneath lowered lashes she watched as the two men argued goodnaturedly over some obscure historical point, and smiled as Gianna leaned across the table towards her and confided with an indulgent shake of her head, 'He should know better than to argue with Angelo. Just as when they play squash together, Angelo always wins!'

Terri said nothing, just smiled again, preferring to keep her thoughts to herself. What Gianna said was undoubtedly true and she had no great difficulty in believing it. But what she found faintly unsettling was the undisguised warmth in the other woman's voice—like the spontaneous affection she had seen earlier in the faces of Peter and Susan Donaldson. Contrary to what she might have wished to believe, there appeared to be no doubt that the Marchese was held in high regard by a considerable section of the community.

She glanced away with a vague sense of confusion. Beneath that popular façade he was still the monster Vicki had warned her against. But a clever, complex, duplicitous monster. One who could switch disguises at the drop of a hat.

As the coffee arrived, Gianna and Leonardo went off to dance. Angelo turned to her as they were left alone. 'That wasn't so painful, was it, *cara*?' He smiled condescendingly. 'I see you're capable of behaving with decorum, after all—when you put your mind to it.'

The truth was she hadn't had to put her mind to it particularly, but, suddenly irritated, she came back at him now, 'One tends to respond to the quality of the company. Fortunately, for once, you were outnumbered.'

He smiled ironically. 'Yes. I guess that was a bonus that both of us enjoyed.'

Terri glared across the table at him. The superficial reign of normality had just been broken, and all she could see before her now was the man who was deliberately standing in her way and preventing her from contacting Ruggero and little Laura. She opened her mouth to return to that subject, but was interrupted as a waiter approached and bent to murmur something in Angelo's ear.

He laid down his napkin and turned to her. 'Excuse me for a couple of minutes. A couple of my guests are leaving. I have to go and see them off.'

Terri nodded and watched him go, concealing the sudden flutter within. This was her perfect chance. While he was busy seeing off his guests, she could take advantage of his absence to do a bit of secret sleuthing. The vital information she needed had to be hidden away here somewhere—and, since he refused to give it freely, she would have to resort to his tactics. Deception, trickery and stealth.

She slipped from her seat and made her way across the balcony, through the huge drawing-room and out into the corridor. She looked around her. There was no sign of Angelo. Then she frowned, mentally struggling to get her bearings. The study where he had entertained her that first time would be on an upper floor, she guessed. And that seemed the most likely place for her to begin her search. Somewhere in some file there were bound to be names and addresses and phone numbers of contacts in Hamburg and Rotterdam.

At the end of the corridor and across the hallway she could see the lift that she had travelled in before. But she couldn't risk taking the lift now—it was too exposed. Instinctively, she doubled back along another corridor, heading in the opposite direction. What she was looking for now were stairs.

At the sound of voices she ducked into a doorway, then held her breath with beating heart as two young men in blue and black uniforms went hurrying past. Then she was scurrying to the end of the corridor, along another passageway, and through the double doors at the end. Her heart leapt. Her instincts had been right. Here was the staircase she had been looking for.

She took the stairs two at a time and, one floor higher, emerged into a narrow passageway, exactly like the one below. The layout of each floor of the old fortress was similar, it seemed. Then she was moving swiftly along another corridor, through a set of arches and out into a blue-tiled hall. She peered at the low divans that were arranged against the walls. This was it! She remembered it well.

The study had to be back through those arches, she decided, dredging her memory. Then a short way along the corridor and the second door on the left.

Her palms were clammy with excitement as she came to the door, pausing to sneak a quick glance at her watch. She had only been gone a matter of minutes. Angelo would not have missed her yet. She reached for the door-handle—and swore. 'Damn!' It was locked.

But don't panic, she told herself. Try the next one. Conveniently adjoining the study, she recalled, was the room where they had had lunch. If she could gain access to that one, all would not be lost.

She couldn't resist a smile of triumph as the handle turned beneath her trembling fingers. She was in luck. Holding her breath, she pushed the door open and stepped into the darkened room. But, as her fingers found the light switch and she closed the door, she stiffened with mingled annoyance and disbelief. This was definitely not the room she was looking for.

It was a huge room, the predominantly silver and black décor lending it an undeniably masculine stamp. And judging by the piece of furniture that totally dominated the floor—an enormous, circular, canopied bed—it was not a room much used for eating or studying. Her sense of direction had quite clearly let her down. She had strayed accidentally into Angelo's bedroom.

Double blast and double damn! Her first instinct was to beat a hasty retreat. She was unlikely to find what she was looking for here. Then a little bedside bureau caught her eye, and a sudden rash impulse stopped her in her tracks. Who knew? Maybe she would find some address book there. It would only take an extra few seconds to look.

It was a fatal few seconds, as it turned out. Even as she turned her back and bent to examine the bureau drawer, behind her, silently, the bedroom door opened and a tall, dark figure in a dinner-suit stepped soundlessly into the room. With an inscrutable expression, he paused to watch as Terri started to fumble with the bureau drawer, then he pushed the bedroom door closed behind him with a sharp and very deliberate click.

The sweat of panic on her brow, Terri swung round startled and stared in dismay. 'Angelo!' was all she could think of to say.

'So,' he regarded her with those piercing black eyes, 'you managed to find your way to my room.'

Oh, lord, what was he thinking? 'I made a mistake,' she started to babble, not liking the way he was eyeing her now, his gaze travelling wantonly to her breasts, then downwards to caress her legs. 'It's not what you . . . I didn't mean to . . .' Dry-mouthed, she started to back away.

He smiled a strange smile. 'Don't apologise, *mia cara*. I'm not complaining.' Then he half turned round to lock the door, took the key carefully from the lock and dropped it into his jacket pocket. 'Though I have to say I'm a little surprised. I had no idea you'd be in such a hurry to do that market research we talked about.'

Terri opened her mouth to protest, but no sound came out. And suddenly her legs were rooted to the spot, paralysed with panic and horror, as on silent, panther-like strides he started to come across the room towards her.

CHAPTER FIVE

THE next moment he was standing over her, a towering, menacing, dark presence, and Terri's heart was fluttering like a half-demented bird in her throat.

'Angelo, I . . . please believe me . . .' She tried to take a step back, away from him, but she was wedged now between the bureau and the bed—that degenerate ocean of black silk beneath its draped and silvered canopy. 'That's not why I'm here.' Her voice was a croak. 'I promise you, that's not why I'm here!'

'No?' He smiled a disbelieving smile and took another step towards her. 'No need to be so shy, Teresa. We're two consenting adults, after all.'

'But you're wrong!' Her limbs felt suddenly stiff and awkward, as though they belonged to someone else. She could feel the coolness of the black silk coverlet pressing against the backs of her legs. 'I'm not . . . please stop . . .' she stammered.

But already he was reaching out to take hold of her, one hand grabbing her by the shoulder, the other sliding round the back of her neck to hold her head firmly in his grasp. The black eyes blazed down into hers. 'Let's not waste time with empty protestations, *mia cara*.' Then, in one movement, he jerked her towards him, the hand on her shoulder roughly pulling aside the flimsy fabric of her top, almost entirely exposing one breast, and she could feel the heat in him as he bent towards her, forcing her lips into contact with his.

At the same instant that his mouth covered hers in an unrelenting, fierce, hard kiss, his fingers slid beneath the cotton of her top to grasp in his palm the swell of her breast.

For one split second Terri seemed to freeze, overwhelmed by this pagan attack on her senses. For in that instant the panic in her fled to be replaced by a new, raw, rich emotion that sent a fire through her loins and a thrill through her veins. The breath left her body as his lips captured hers and her limbs seemed to turn to water as she felt his body press against hers, hard and demanding, sensuous and warm. And, just for a moment, her senses betrayed her as, with a sigh almost of surrender, she allowed him to prise her lips apart.

Then panic overtook her again—though it was fear of the treachery in her own trembling lips now more than any fear of him—and with a sudden Amazonian burst of strength she struggled to free herself from him. But the effort was totally self-defeating. As she struggled, she lost her balance and found herself sprawling backwards across the bed—with Angelo on top of her.

His face was mere centimetres from hers as he looked down at her, his expression taunting. 'Why, Teresa? There's no need for all this. Why put up a fight? Why pretend to resist?' His body pinned her to the black silk coverlet as he bent to claim her lips once more. 'A hot-blooded Englishwoman like yourself . . . just lie back and relax. You'll enjoy it more that way.'

But the panic in her was growing now. As his hand slid downwards once more to cover her breast, she began to pummel him with her fists, raining down blows on the broad, hard shoulders, the rock-solid contours of his arms and chest with every puny ounce of her strength.

'Let me go! How dare you, you bastard?' She tore her mouth away from his. 'I didn't come here for this! I got the wrong room . . . I thought it was your study. All I wanted was to see if I could find some address or phone number for Ruggero!'

His expression changed. 'I see,' he said. Then he slid from the bed to stand over her again. And there was something in the caustic smile that brushed his lips as he adjusted the black bow-tie at his throat that told her he had known that all along. 'So, you thought you'd try and outsmart me, *mia cara*. That, as I could have warned you, was not a sensible thing to do. Very few people outsmart me, Teresa, and I fear you're not destined to be one of them.'

As she hastily struggled to gather herself, slithering across the bed away from him, adjusting the still-gaping front of her top, he paused to regard her dishevelled state with a cool, superior smile. 'Perhaps that will serve to teach you a lesson. Straying into strange men's bedrooms can prove to be a risky pursuit.'

Terri threw him a hard, unforgiving look. Hadn't

he just made a very thorough job of demonstrating the truth of that? Her mouth was still tingling, hot and bruised, her blood pumping madly through her veins. 'Yes,' she agreed with venom, 'I think you've adequately made your point.'

'Good.' With a deliberate gesture, Angelo reached into his jacket pocket and withdrew the key. Then, with Terri following at a safe distance behind him, he started to move towards the door. Carefully he slid the key in the lock and with a quick click the door was opened.

He turned to smile at her. 'Till later.' Then, almost before she realised what was happening, he had stepped out into the corridor and closed the door again.

Aghast, Terri rushed forward, just as the lock clicked on the other side. Furiously she banged on the door. 'What the hell do you think you're doing?'

There was cruel amusement in the voice that answered her. 'Surely you didn't think I was going to let you off so lightly? For the moment, you stay there.' He paused before adding with undisguised relish, 'Until I decide on your punishment.'

Terri battered the door with her fists. 'Let me out! You have no right!'

But he merely answered, 'Make all the noise you want. No one will hear you. And besides, no one can release you but me. I have the key safely in my pocket.'

Then, oblivious to her bangs and yells, she heard his footsteps retreat along the corridor.

Terri raged till she almost foamed at the mouth. How dared he have the audacity to make a prisoner of her? Though, unwillingly, she had to acknowledge that she had brought her misfortune on herself. She should have known better than to try to trick him. Trickery was his speciality, not hers. Though fate, it seemed, had tricked her too. Of all the scores of rooms in the Casa Grande, why did she have to go stumbling straight into Angelo's bedroom?

And there appeared to be no way out. A french window on one wall led out on to a narrow balcony from which she could just dimly hear the sounds of music and laughter coming from the floor below. The part of the old fortress where the party was being held was on the other side. She could shout with all the strength of her lungs and nobody would hear her. Angelo had been right about that.

She considered the possibility of an Alcatraz-style escape. She could knot together the king-size black sheets and tie them to the balcony. But she instantly rejected the idea. The way things were going for her tonight, she would probably end up breaking her neck!

Likewise, the en-suite bathroom and walk-in closet offered no hope. She was, as he had pointed out, totally and utterly at his mercy.

She seated herself nervously in a black and silver-upholstered armchair, studiously avoiding the vast, canopied bed, and glanced impatiently at her watch. It was just after midnight. The party could go on for hours yet. How long did he plan on keeping her here?

And more to the point, she fretted, recalling with a warm flush his earlier assault, what manner of 'punishment' did he have in store for her?

And again she cursed herself for her own foolishness. Had she been wiser, just a little more cautious, she would never have ended up in this mess.

About two hours later, exhausted from the anxiety of waiting, she dropped off and slept fitfully for an hour or so, reawakening with a hideous crick in her neck. She stumbled to the balcony and listened. Downstairs all was quiet now. The party had evidently broken up. She turned back, her eyes on the door, feeling her stomach shrink. Now, any minute, Angelo would appear and take pleasure in pronouncing her fate.

But another half-hour passed as she paced nervously up and down the room, and still there was no sign of him. She went back to the armchair and slumped down, hating him with all her strength. Every muscle in her body ached, every sinew was crying out for sleep—and the big black bed with its rumpled coverlet looked so cool, so inviting. But she would not, could not bring herself to cross the room and stretch out on it. That was the last place she wanted Angelo to find her when he finally came walking through the door.

And still she waited. And still he did not come. Exhausted, still cursing him, she drifted into uneasy sleep.

When the key finally did grate in the lock, Terri awakened instantly. She sat upright with a start, feeling dull and groggy with sleep. The room was bathed in a warm golden light. She peered at her watch. It was nine o'clock.

The first thing to appear round the door was a trolley—laden with covered dishes and steaming pots of coffee and milk. Then, at the other end of it, a tall, dark figure in a black silk robe, jet-dark hair sleek and glossy from the shower, a stubble of beard round his jaw and chin.

'Good morning, Teresa. I hope you slept well.' He paused to bestow a sadistic smile before, very pointedly, relocking the door and slipping the key into the pocket of his robe. 'I thought you might be hungry. I've brought you some breakfast.'

Terri struggled from her seat, her body aching from top to toe as though she had spent the night in a threshing machine. She glared resentfully at him. 'You could have saved yourself the trouble. I don't want any breakfast. All I want is for you, *this minute*, to let me out of here.'

Angelo shook his head with mock regret. 'Sorry, Teresa, that's not the plan.' With a wicked smile he patted the pocket of his robe. 'Unless, of course, you want to have a go at taking the key from me yourself?'

Involuntarily she took a step back. That was the last thing she was likely to do. It was perfectly obvious, even to her untrained eye, that he was wearing nothing beneath the thin robe. She deliberately kept her eyes on his face, her arms folded protectively across her chest, and blotted from her vision the tantalising triangle of dark-tanned flesh that showed above the V of the loosely tied robe. In a tight voice she demanded, 'What are you doing here, anyway, if you haven't come to let me out?'

'I told you, I've brought you breakfast.'

'And I don't want it, so you might as well go.'

He carried on, ignoring her. 'I also brought you this.' He took from the handle of the trolley a couple of wire hangers covered in plastic and tossed them casually on to the bed. 'A change of clothes. I thought you might need them—after sitting up all night.' A taunting smile curled round his lips. 'There was no need to stand on ceremony, you know. You should have used the bed. I assure you, it's most comfortable.'

Terri shot him another harsh look, then told him, almost primly, 'I'm afraid I don't make a habit of sleeping in strange men's beds.'

'Even when the strange man in question is sleeping like a baby in another room?'

'I didn't know that, did I?'

'So you thought I might come back?'

As he paused to let his eyes glide over her face, his expression baiting, sardonically amused, Terri understood in a flash what the nature of her punishment had been—to be left in a state of anxiety all night, not knowing if or when he might appear. As she opened her mouth to speak her mind—the man was a sadist!—he cut in, 'So sorry to have disappointed you, *cara*. That bit of market research of yours will have to wait for some other time. In the meantime,' he added, smoothly changing the subject as she glowered angrily at him, 'do you want to use the bathroom first—or shall I?'

For a moment Terri was thrown. 'What are you talking about?' she demanded. 'I just want you to let me out of here!'

He shrugged. 'OK, I'll go first. I've already showered, but I haven't shaved. I won't be long.' He smiled blandly. 'Have some breakfast while you're waiting.'

Helpless with fury, Terri could only stand and watch as he disappeared into the bathroom and closed the door. He was making her pay for her mistake, all right. And he was enjoying every second of his revenge.

Without appetite, she glanced at the trolley—at the scrambled eggs and croissants and hot, buttered toast—then poured herself a glass of orange juice and drank. After the rigours of the night her mouth felt dry and stale—but her stomach was still too tense for food. Then, trying to ignore the cheerful humming and the sounds of splashing water coming from next door, she paced restlessly up and down the floor, feeling like an animal imprisoned in a cage.

As the bathroom door clicked open at last, she positioned herself by the locked exit door. Then, as Angelo came into the room, she told him tersely, 'I'm waiting to be let out.'

It was as though she hadn't spoken. He threw an indifferent smile at her. 'OK, your turn now. While you're in there, I'll get dressed.'

She didn't move. 'Look, I'm sick of this charade.

Just unlock the door and let me go.'

Still he was deaf to her demands. Without even a glance at her, he disappeared into the wardrobe and emerged a couple of minutes later with a pile of clothes slung over his arm. She watched him lay them out calmly on the bed—shirt, trousers, underwear, socks—and felt her blood begin to boil. He was deliberately ignoring her, treating her with contempt. She said, more loudly, 'Please open the door!'

At last he turned to look at her, one eyebrow arching as he spoke. 'Why don't you go and use the bathroom now? I'd like to get dressed.'

'Let me go and you can do what you want.'

'I'll do what I want anyway.' As his hand reached for the belt of his robe, he threw an openly provocative smile. 'If you want to stick around and watch, you're more than welcome to.'

'You wouldn't . . .'

He shrugged. 'Suit yourself.' Then in one fluid movement the belt was undone and the dark robe began to slither to the floor.

Before it ever got there, Terri had plunged across the room, into the bathroom and locked the door. Her cheeks were crimson. Her heart was beating fast. As deliberately low-down tactics went, that had definitely been below the belt!

However, now that she was in the bathroom she decided she might as well take a shower. She felt sticky and uncomfortable after spending all night in her party clothes. Then, as she caught sight of herself in the mirror, she realised she looked even worse than

she felt. Her skirt and top were crumpled like rags,
her hair half-in and half-out of its plait. No wonder
Angelo had smiled when he had seen her! The
restless, sleepless night she had spent was written as
plain as the nose on her face.

She switched on the shower and began to undress,
then remembered the change of clothes he had
brought. She tapped on the door to draw his attention,
then called through, without opening up, 'Those
things you brought . . . Please, would you mind
passing them through?'

There was a pause. 'Come out and get them,' he
told her.

'I will not.' For all she knew, he might still be
standing there half naked.

Another pause, then she jumped back nervously
from the door as there was a click against the door-
handle on the other side. 'There you are,' she heard
him say. 'All you have to do is reach out and take
them.'

Gingerly she opened the door a crack and, keeping
her eyes carefully averted, reached out one hand to
grope for the pair of hangers that were suspended
from the door-handle. Then she instantly snatched
her arm back inside, as though afraid that he might
grab her. Though she knew that was a ridiculous
notion. Last night he might have given her a
deliberate fright in order to teach her a salutary
lesson, but Angelo was scarcely the type of man who
made a habit of forcing himself on defenceless young
women. Judging by what she had seen last night,

women were more likely to force themselves on him!

Carefully, she relocked the door and pulled the plastic covers from the hangers. A stylish pair of ladies' white trousers and a pretty coral blouse were revealed. Plus, dangling from the neck of one of the hangers, a pair of brand-new, flat-heeled sandals. So he had thought of everything. Terri frowned ironically to herself as she hung the hangers on the back of the door, stripped off and dived beneath the shower. Of course he had thought of everything. When did he ever not?

Five minutes later, as she rubbed herself dry with one of the huge, soft black and white towels, Terri was starting to feel half human again. She even looked semi-presentable, she decided, as she dressed quickly, then unbraided her shoulder-length hair and brushed it into a billow of waves. The outfit was fresh and flattering, and the loose, soft hairstyle helped to camouflage the lines of fatigue that still lingered in her face.

The transformation was reflected in Angelo's look of appreciation as a moment later she emerged through the door—though he restricted himself verbally to the impartial observation. 'Good. I see they fit.'

He was seated on the edge of the bed, fully dressed, she was relieved to see, in a pair of light blue trousers and a blue checked shirt, open at the neck, the sleeves rolled back casually at the wrists. He had pulled the breakfast trolley alongside him and was helping himself to a slice of toast.

'Perfectly,' she told him, hovering, not quite certain where to put herself. 'That was exceedingly thoughtful of you. And so convenient,' she couldn't resist adding, 'that you should just happen to have them lying around.'

Angelo raised his coffee-cup unhurriedly and eyed her over the top of it. 'Oh, they weren't just lying around,' he assured her. 'I had them sent over. They belong to my sister, in case you're wondering.'

'Your sister?' She revealed her surprise—for it had of course crossed her mind to wonder, and the conclusion she had drawn had been somewhat different. 'I assumed they'd been left behind by one of your many lady friends.' She was still hovering, irritated by the smile on his face. 'I couldn't help but notice at the party . . . That's quite a little harem you've got.'

'Harem?' He seemed amused by her choice of word. Then he added, observing her tight-lipped face, 'I take it that you disapprove?'

'Disapprove?' Terri shrugged elaborately. What did she care about his private life? It was not of the slightest interest to her the number of women he possessed—nor the frequency with which they passed between the black silk sheets. But she couldn't quite resist the temptation to point out, her tone ironical, sarcastic, 'I might be just a little surprised. From the way you so liberally slandered my sister, I took you to be a man of high moral principles.' She paused, fixing him with a steely blue eye. 'Perhaps, like so many men, you conveniently employ double standards when it comes to personal morality.'

He continued to watch her as he bit into the toast. The black eyes scrutinised her face. 'Even if your assumptions about me were true, morally, there would be a world of difference between my behaviour and that of your sister.'

'Why?' Terri pounced on him. 'Because she's a woman and you're a man?'

A brief smile softened the sudden harshness of his face. 'I agree, there is that, of course.' Then the smile fled as he continued, 'But considerably more to the point, I'd say, is the fact that she is married, whereas I am not.'

As Terri met the hostile gaze, she was struck by the total condemnation in his eyes. A condemnation, she could sense, that came right from the heart of him. And suddenly there was no doubt in her mind that he believed every word he had told her about Vicki. He had not, as she had once accused him, simply invented the stories in order to blacken her sister's name.

As she lowered her eyes, doubt flickered inside her. Was it possible, after all, that there might be some truth in his slanderous claims?

Since her emergence from the bathroom, Terri had remained on her feet, disinclined to give the impression that she was anything other than anxious to leave. Now, at last, Angelo started to stand up too, and she heaved an inward sigh of relief. It looked as if her release was imminent. But he instantly dashed her hopes as he told her, 'I'm going now, but I'll leave the trolley. I think you should have something to eat.' As she gaped at him in horror, uncomprehending, he added, 'I don't expect to be back till evening.'

'What?' Terri's mouth fell open. 'Surely now you're going to let me go?'

'*Mi dispiace.* I'm sorry.' Solemnly he shook his head. 'I can't have you running all over the island questioning the inhabitants any more. You leave me no alternative, *mia cara*, but to keep you under lock and key.'

'But you can't—you can't keep me prisoner! You've no right to do that!'

'Even less can I take the risk of your spreading rumours and gossip about my family round the island. I warned you to tread carefully, but you grow more reckless with every day. I'm sorry, Teresa, I cannot allow it.'

'What if I promised to stay at home?' The truth was, she was feeling far too tired to do much sleuthing today, and she had already decided to wait until Monday to continue her investigations. Then she would act on an inspiration that had come to her in the middle of the night, and that she had cursed herself for not thinking of before—she would phone Ruggero's secretary at the Montefalcone office and see what she could winkle out of her. 'Just take me back to the villa,' she implored now. 'I promise I'll go straight to bed.'

But Angelo showed no signs of relenting. He stood over her and shook his head. 'I'm sorry, Teresa, but I can't trust you. You've already made that very plain.'

'You can this time.' And, for once, it was true. 'I

give you my word I won't leave the house.'

'No, *mia cara*, I regret . . .'

'But you can't keep me locked up here!'

Angelo paused and seemed to think for a moment. 'There may just be an alternative.' The dark eyes narrowed. 'You could accompany me. Up on Falcon Mountain where I'm going, not even you could get into mischief.' He smiled a cautionary smile. 'And one thing's absolutely sure—there's no way you could give me the slip.'

Terri regarded him with suspicion, not caring in the least for this latest proposition. An outing to Falcon Mountain in his company was almost as unappealing as remaining locked up here. She hesitated, and made one final pitch at trying to turn him round. 'I promise this time you can trust me. Take me back to the villa and I'll just go to bed for the day.'

He shook his head impatiently and started to turn away. 'OK, you've made your choice. You remain here under lock and key.'

'No, please!' She started to hurry after him with a sudden sense of panic. 'Please don't lock me up again. I couldn't bear to be shut in all day!'

He paused. 'Then you'd prefer to come with me?'

Terri sighed. 'Prefer' was scarcely an appropriate word. It was a choice between the Devil and the deep blue sea. But as he started to move towards the door again she took a deep breath and scurried after him.

Just this once, she would opt for the Devil. 'OK,' she told him, 'I'll go with you.'

CHAPTER SIX

HALF an hour later they were heading up a narrow, twisting mountain road, leaving the rest of the island far below.

Terri sat back in the soft leather bucket seat of the Ferrari and resigned herself to the fact that she was still very much Angelo's prisoner. They had passed only two cars on the way, the last one more than half an hour ago. As he had already pointed out to her, it would be a waste of time trying to give him the slip up here. Unless, of course, she fancied a long, uncomfortable trek back on foot. Which, in her current state of fatigue, she most certainly did not.

At last they turned off the main road on to an even narrower bumpy track, then through a set of tall iron gates to park in the shade of a big open courtyard.

'This is it,' Angelo told her. 'This is where our precious falcons are kept.'

A wiry little man in dirty farm clothes came hurrying towards them, his craggy face abeam. 'This is Amilcare,' Angelo introduced her. 'He's in charge of all the birds here.' Then to Amilcare, 'Teresa, a young friend from England. She's most interested in the work you do here.' He glanced across at Terri again. 'I take it you are interested? If not, you can always just sit in the car.'

It had crossed Terri's mind to do just that—as a demonstration of what an unwilling companion she was. But the clear mountain air had revived her a bit, and it seemed like rather a waste just to sulk. She smiled at Amilcare, ignoring Angelo. 'I'd love to see your birds,' she said.

She followed the two men across the courtyard, then along past a low, rough-walled building. 'The mews,' Angelo told her over his shoulder. 'Where the falcons are kept at night.' Then Amilcare paused before what appeared to be a small, square window cut into the wall. '*Guardi, signore,*' he invited as Angelo bent to take a look inside.

Curiously, Terri watched as Angelo nodded and smiled, then made some remark in Italian to Amilcare before turning at last to her. 'Take a look, Teresa,' he told her. 'Tell me what you see.'

At first, all she could make out in one corner of the big, well-lit cage beyond the glass was a crouching, speckle-breasted bird. 'It's a falcon,' she offered.

'And?'

She peered closer—then she saw them. She smiled with pleasure. 'She's sitting on some eggs!'

'Four eggs, to be precise, and due to hatch any day now.' Angelo smiled proudly. 'It'll be our second hatching this year. No mean feat,' he added with a deferential little nod in the direction of Amilcare. 'Breeding falcons in captivity is no easy task.'

Terri followed with growing interest as the tour around the mews continued, listening uncomprehendingly to the constant exchanges between the two men, yet understanding, at least, that there existed between the two a bond of friendship and mutual respect—and that she was witnessing a side to Angelo that she had not glimpsed before. A totally relaxed and uncynical side. Boyishly enthusiastic. Unselfconsciously caring.

He turned to her with a mysterious smile. 'Now I'd like you to meet Khan,' he said.

In single file they made their way to the end of the mews till they came to another, smaller courtyard, one corner shaded from the sun. And there, perched on a low wooden block stuck in the ground, a grey-brown bird was watching them.

Terri stood well back and regarded the creature with some hesitation. The strong-looking yellow beak curved to a vicious hook. The merciless, black, unblinking eyes. 'I thought you kept them all in cages,' she said.

Angelo smiled and shook his head. 'There is no need,' he assured her. 'If you look at his feet, you can see he is tethered. There is no way that he can fly away.'

That the bird might fly away was not at that moment what was on Terri's mind. Her principal concern was just to keep a respectable distance between it and herself.

Angelo, evidently, had no such misgivings. She watched with fascination as Amilcare now handed his boss a heavy leather gauntlet, of the type she had seen falconers wear, and Angelo slipped it on. Then, with total confidence, he crossed to the bird, freed it from its perch and allowed it to step on to his gloved wrist.

With his free hand he gently caressed the bird's pale-speckled breast, letting the backs of his fingers move softly over the gleaming feathers. He told her with pride in his voice, 'Not only is Khan our best breeding male—the father of the chicks that are due to hatch—but he's also a champion hunter. I trained him myself.'

The bird seemed remarkably still on his wrist, yet as Angelo started to come towards her Terri felt a tightening in the pit of her stomach. She smiled awkwardly. 'He looks very fierce,' she said.

'Don't worry.' Angelo was reassuring. 'I have him firmly by the leash. And besides, he's not as fierce as he looks. You're perfectly safe. Unlike man, the falcon does not attack for pleasure, only in order to feed itself.' He paused and added with humour, 'And Khan, I promise you, Teresa, has been recently fed.'

She met the twinkle in his eye and felt herself begin to relax. Close to, the bird was smaller than she had expected—less than thirty centimetres high—and there was a still composure about its bearing that was faintly reassuring somehow. Besides, she knew instinctively that she could trust Angelo. If he said she was safe, then she could take it that she was. She glanced up at him. 'He's very beautiful,' she confessed.

He nodded. 'A bird like this, in some parts of the

world, would fetch many tens of thousands of dollars. He's a peregrine, the prince of falcons.' He held the bird out to her. 'Stroke him,' he told her. 'See how tame he really is.'

Tentatively, Terri reached out.

'Use the back of your fingers.'

'Like this?' She touched her fingers against the feathers, faintly surprised at the softness, the warmth. The bird's black eyes were watching her, unthreatening, yet supremely alert.

'Would you like to hold him?'

She shifted her eyes back to Angelo, feeling a *frisson* of danger, not certain if she dared.

'Don't worry, I'll be watching over you.'

She paused a moment longer, then nodded. 'OK,' she agreed.

Angelo turned to the wiry Amilcare and instructed him to bring another glove. Then he turned back to Terri. 'Keep stroking him,' he urged. 'Get to know him. Let him get to know you.'

A moment later Amilcare reappeared, carrying the glove, and she slipped it on. It was of soft, supple buckskin, yet thick to protect against razor-sharp talons. And, she was pleased to note, it came half-way up her arm.

'Now hold your hand out, palm downwards, fist clenched. Keep your movements slow and steady. You are the master, remember. You must inspire confidence in the bird.'

She held out her hand.

He moved towards her, his gloved hand coming

alongside hers. All the while, he spoke to the bird, his voice low and reassuring, coaxing. And she could sense the deep, instinctive communication between man and bird.

'*Piano* . . . steady . . .'

She kept her eyes fixed on the bird as, with a slight flutter of its wings, just enough to enable it to keep its balance, it took a sudden, decisive hop on to the wrist of her glove.

Involuntarily, Terri felt a surge of triumph. A pleased grin spread across her face.

'Well done!' Angelo was watching her. 'That's right,' he nodded. 'Keep stroking him.'

The weight of the falcon was less than she had expected, the grip of the steely talons light against her protected arm. As her fingers caressed the soft, silky feathers, Angelo continued to stand at her side, the leash attached to the falcon's feet held lightly in his hand. And for a moment Terri was aware of a strange, fierce bond between the three of them—the powerful, dark-eyed man, the falcon and herself. For one fleeting, primal instant the three of them were one.

Then the instant passed.

'Would you like to see him fly?' Angelo asked.

She nodded, avoiding his eyes, wondering if he had felt the same thing, too. 'I'd love to,' she replied.

It was an extraordinary experience. They drove in an open farm truck to a high, secluded spot that overlooked the valley. Behind them, Falcon Mountain, bathed now in bright sunlight; before them, off in the distance, an endless stretch of shimmering blue sea. For the journey the falcon wore a purple leather hood with pink and blue plumes. 'To keep him tranquil,' Angelo explained. Then they were on the edge of the cliff, and in a moment of sheer exquisiteness the bird was unhooded and released, rising on effortless wings into the empty, clear blue sky.

In an awakening of wonderment, Terri watched as it swooped and soared, the broad wings that carried it higher and higher touched by pure gold from the sun.

'Beautiful, huh?' Angelo was at her side.

She nodded. 'It's breathtaking.'

She felt him smile. He touched her arm. 'I can see we're converting you,' he said.

Later they drove to a quiet spot and lay on the warm grass eating salami-filled rolls and drinking red wine from the picnic hamper Amilcare had thoughtfully prepared for them.

'*Salute*!' Angelo raised his glass to her.

'Cheers!' Terri smiled back at him and watched through lowered lashes as he drank, aware of the two conflicting urges that were battling inside her. The urge to relax with him and just enjoy his company—which, in spite of herself, she realised would not be so difficult a task. And the opposite, more ingrained urge to keep her defences up. She turned uneasily away to gaze for a moment out over the landscape. Then she glanced across at him again as he leaned casually against the bole of a tree.

'How does it feel to look out over all this and know that it belongs to you?' she asked.

He smiled and leaned back his head, regarding her through candid dark eyes. 'It feels like an enormous privilege—and also something of a responsibility.'

She continued to watch him, her eyes on his face, aware of a new openness she saw there. 'You must have been quite young when you inherited the title?' she asked.

'I was just twenty-two. My father was killed in a helicopter crash.'

'Yes.' She had heard about the death of his father, the old Marchese, from Vicki. She glanced down at her wine and confided, 'I was fifteen when my father died.'

'So we have something in common.'

Terri gave a light, ironical laugh. 'You think so?' They might both have been left fatherless at a relatively young age, but in wildly different circumstances. 'Unlike you, I inherited no island and no title. Just a penniless, grief-stricken mother and an over-dependent younger sister.'

Angelo watched her. 'Is your mother still alive?'

'Oh, yes.' She nodded. 'Alive and well. Since Vicki got married she's lived with her sister down in Bristol. I go down to see her whenever I can.' She looked up at him through narrowed eyes. 'Your own family is rather larger, I understand.'

He smiled. 'I have three sisters and three brothers—aside from Ruggero who, as you know, is really my cousin.'

Quite a clan! Terri smiled knowingly to herself as she took a mouthful from her glass. No wonder poor Vicki had felt beleaguered at times with all those in-laws breathing down her neck!

As though reading her mind, Angelo said with a smile, 'Large families are something of a tradition in Sicily. Apart from my mother, however, only one sister still lives on the island. The rest of them are scattered in different parts of Italy.'

Terri couldn't resist a good-natured gibe. 'They were no doubt anxious to escape from your big-brotherly supervision!'

He smiled. 'Perhaps you're right. Or perhaps their destinies just lay elsewhere.' He paused. 'I've always known that mine lay here. Through the generations there must always be Montefalcones on Santa Pietrina.'

Through the generations. He was referring, of course, to his own heirs. Given the relaxed, confidential mood that reigned, Terri decided to risk a personal question. 'Why aren't you married?' she asked. 'Oughtn't you to be producing heirs?'

He held her eyes. 'Don't worry, *mia cara*. I intend to produce many.' Then, still watching her, he leaned back and answered her question with a faintly self-derisory smile. 'It's the old story, I suppose. I haven't met the right girl yet.'

Terri looked disbelieving. 'Even with such a wide choice available?' she scoffed.

He laughed at that. 'You mean my harem?' Then his expression sobered as he went on, '*Cara* Teresa, it is not the size of the field that is important, but the quality.' He paused for a moment and held her eyes. 'In one form or another, *mia cara*, we have all experienced our Steves.'

Terri felt something inside her tighten at the total unexpectedness of the remark. It had been spoken, she could not help but sense, with open, artless honesty. Almost as a gesture of solidarity. She looked across at Angelo and seemed to catch a glimpse of the unguarded inner man. Was it really possible, she wondered, that he too could have experienced disappointment in love? Was the Marchese Angelo de Montefalcone an ordinary mortal, after all?

With an uneasy stab she glanced away. There were so many unseen sides to him. He was as full of contrasts and surprises as the wild, rugged landscape that surrounded them.

It seemed no time at all before the sun began to sink. They drove back to the farm to pick up the Ferrari, then made their way down the mountain road, not talking much, but in a silence that was almost companionable. As Terri leaned back in her seat, feeling relaxed and pleasantly sleepy, she was forced to confess to herself that the day had not turned out to be the ghastly ordeal she had expected, after all. In fact, the bizarre truth was that she had actually quite enjoyed herself.

As Angelo dropped her off at the villa, she paused, one hand on the car door. 'What about tomorrow?' she asked, half teasing, half in challenge. 'Are you planning to come and take me prisoner again?'

He turned round slowly to meet her eyes. 'We'll think about tomorrow when it comes, *mia cara*. But don't worry, I'll be keeping an eye on you. In the meantime, I suggest you get some rest.'

She paused on the terrace to watch him go, feeling oddly mellow, at peace with the world. A warm bath, then bed, she decided. A quiet end to a bewildering day.

She was not prepared for the shock that awaited her as she walked into the sitting-room to find Vicki waiting for her there.

'Vicki! Why didn't you tell me you were coming?'

With a gasp of mingled pleasure and surprise, Terri hurried across the room to embrace her. Then, affectionately, she took her sister's arm and drew her down on the sofa beside her, suddenly feeling her heart contract as she looked into the other girl's eyes. The lines of unhappiness and tension that she had seen in London had scored themselves more deeply into the once carefree and childlike face. She looked thinner too, pale and drawn, her fingers toying nervously with the hem of her yellow dress.

She looked at Terri. 'I had to come. Not knowing, just waiting, was getting me down.' The dulled eyes in the pinched face frowned. 'You were with Angelo—I saw the car.' Nervously she licked dry lips. 'Has he relented yet? Has he told you where Ruggero is?'

With a deep sigh, Terri shook her head. 'He's

refusing to budge one inch, I'm afraid.' Then she added quickly, as Vicki's face fell, 'But I managed to get something out of Enzo Tardelli. He said Ruggero mentioned a business trip to Hamburg. Or maybe Rotterdam—he wasn't sure.' Excitedly she squeezed Vicki's arm. 'There must be some way we could get in touch with him there. I was thinking of phoning his secretary tomorrow—unless you can help. You must know who his contacts are there.'

Dolefully Vicki shook her head. 'I never went with him to either of these places—and I already thought about his secretary, I'm afraid. I tried to phone her the other day, but I was told she's gone off on holiday. And there's no one else in the office who can help.'

'Damn!' Terri hated to admit it, but Ruggero's secretary had been her last card.

Vicki was staring down at her hands, still fiddling with the hem of her dress. 'Ruggero never mentioned any business trip to me. Enzo knows more about him than I do, it seems.' A tear slid slowly down her cheek. 'Oh, what a mess I've made of things!'

Terri felt herself stiffen. 'What do you mean?' she asked.

There was a long silence, then Vicki raised her eyes, red-rimmed, tear-filled, brimming with misery. 'Don't tell me Angelo hasn't already told you?' she challenged in a shaky voice.

Terri knew then what was coming—the truth that for some time now she had been starting to dread. But she had to hear it from Vicki's own lips. 'Told me what?' she parried, feeling suddenly cold.

There was another long silence, then Vicki sighed. 'I really screwed things up,' she said. Then she sighed again, and Terri could feel the pain it cost her as, in a small voice, she confessed, 'I committed the ultimate sin. I had an affair with another man.'

Deep inside her, Terri winced. She had been hoping against hope that her fears were wrong. She reached out shakily and took Vicki's hand. 'Why, for pity's sake?' she wanted to know.

For a long moment Vicki seemed unable to speak. Like a child, she clutched at her sister's hand. Her voice barely audible, at last she answered, 'It was because I was so unhappy. Ruggero was away from home so much. At first I started out accepting the occasional invitation to dinner. *Just* dinner,' she emphasised. 'I suppose I did it to spite Ruggero. I thought if he got to hear about it, he might realise he was neglecting me.'

She paused to brush her face with her hand as the tears flowed freely now. 'But he didn't. He didn't seem to realise what was going on.' She paused again. 'Then I met——' Her voice choked on a helpless sob. She shook her head. 'I must have taken leave of my senses—I never meant things to go so far.' Still sobbing, she blinked at Terri. 'I've never loved any man but Ruggero.'

Terri's heart was heavy inside her. It was all exactly as Angelo had said. And suddenly, too, she understood her sister's cryptic phone message that time: 'When you see Ruggero, tell him I'm sorry.' Only it had not just been some silly squabble that she had been apologising for. She slipped an arm round the sob-racked shoulders. 'Oh, Vicki,' was all she could think of to say.

Vicki continued through her sobs. 'Ruggero went crazy when he found out. We had this dreadful, dreadful row. He told me he hated me. He threatened to throw me out. I thought he was going to tear the house down. In the end, I couldn't stand it. I told him I was going back to England and taking Laura with me. That made him even madder, and in the end I had to escape. So I took the car and went for a drive—just to give him time to cool down.' Her voice broke. 'But when I got back to the house, he'd taken Laura and gone.'

Terri sighed with understanding. The whole dismal story made sense at last. Ruggero, the doting father, had simply snatched his little daughter to prevent her being taken off to England. She frowned as she smoothed her sister's hair. 'How did Ruggero find out about the affair?'

'One of his friends. He'd seen us together.'

'It wasn't Angelo who tipped him off?'

Vicki shook her short-cropped head. 'No, it wasn't him.'

For some reason Terri was glad to hear that. But she had to ask, 'Why did you tell me in the beginning that it was all Angelo's fault?'

Vicki wiped her face with the back of her hand. 'I was too ashamed to tell you the truth—I thought you might refuse to help.' Then she added with a defensive sniff, 'Besides, Angelo didn't exactly help things between us. He ruled Ruggero's life. Ruggero listened more to Angelo than he ever did to me.' Her voice broke as she clung to Terri. 'Oh, Terri, my whole life is in ruins! I've lost my husband, I've lost my baby. I don't even know where my baby is!'

Terri soothed her. 'At least she's safe, I'm sure of that.' And it was true—she was. Angelo might have refused to co-operate, but she knew with total certainty that he would allow no harm to come to the child.

She unwrapped her sister's arms from her neck and forced her to look into her eyes. 'Tonight,' she told her calmly, 'you'll stay here with me. Then, first thing tomorrow, we'll go together to speak to Angelo. You must tell him what you've told me—and convince him, as you've convinced me, that you're sorry for what you did.'

Vicki let out a protesting moan. 'I can't! I can't face Angelo.'

Terri shook her. 'You must,' she insisted. Then she held her sister tight for a moment and vowed, 'And this time, one way or another, we're going to get some answers out of him!'

Straight after breakfast next morning, the two girls drove up to the Casa Grande.

Vicki was still highly nervous about the confrontation ahead. 'We really ought to have made an appointment,' she pointed out for the umpteenth time. 'Angelo doesn't like people just barging in on him.'

'That's just too bad.' Terri was adamant. 'It's high time this mystery was cleared up.' Then, as they reached the main entrance and turned into the courtyard with the softly splashing fountain, she urged her sister, 'Don't be nervous. Just concentrate on what you're going to say to him.'

At the heavy, carved main door they were met by a stiff-backed manservant in the familiar blue and black uniform. Then they were invited to wait in the hall while he disappeared off to an internal phone for a quick consultation with the Marchese.

As Vicki pulled an anxious face, Terri exhorted her, 'Chin up!' Remember, the sooner you can convince Angelo, the sooner you'll see Laura and Ruggero again.'

A moment later the servant reappeared and led the two girls to the lift. As Terri watched him press the button—for the *second* floor, she noticed with chagrin!—inwardly she sighed with relief. So far so good. At least Angelo had consented to see them.

He was seated behind his desk, his back to the shutterless window, a blindingly fierce rectangle of light. As Terri stepped ahead of her sister into the room, she blinked at the sudden brightness—and, quite involuntarily, felt a slight tightening in the pit of her stomach at the sight of him. He was dressed in a stark white shirt, almost luminous in the bright light, his features half in shadow, the black hair wreathed in a halo-like glow. Like some dark demi-god awaiting the supplications of his minions.

Mentally, she pulled herself up. This was no

celestial being, no angel—in spite of his name.

Angelo spoke first. He said in a cool tone, addressing himself to Terri, 'I wasn't aware we'd made an appointment for this hour?'

'We haven't.' Terri's tone was equally cool. She felt Vicki wince slightly at her side. 'Since we're here on family business, I assumed an appointment wouldn't be necessary.' She held his eyes. 'However, if I'm wrong and you have matters of a business nature that you feel should take precedence, we'd be more than happy to leave you and come back some other time.' She made a movement as though to turn and leave. 'We would hate to impose on you for something so trivial when you have more important things on your mind.'

As her eyes grew accustomed to the light, she thought she saw a faint smile cross his lips. 'That won't be necessary,' he said. 'Since you're already here, I'll spare you a minute or two of my time.'

'How kind.' With a gesture of mock-acquiescence, Terri turned back again, feeling rather pleased with herself for the way she had handled that. Then she added for good measure, 'Just so long as you're absolutely sure that we're not intruding . . .'

Angelo tossed the pen in his hand to one side and indicated the pair of brocade-upholstered, straight-backed chairs that faced him across the desk. 'So let's hear what you've come for, shall we?' As though he didn't know!

She sat, inviting Vicki to do the same, and met the dark gaze levelly. Not once, she noted angrily, had he even so much as glanced at her sister. It was almost as though she wasn't there. She indicated the silent figure with a brief wave of her hand. 'We've come about Ruggero and Laura. To demand that you reveal to us where they are.'

'Demand?' He raised a dark eyebrow at her. There was a slight inflection in his tone.

'Yes, demand.' She was not about to be intimidated now. 'You have no right to keep this information from my sister. It is her right to be told where her husband is holding their child.' Before he could interrupt, she hurried on, 'And it is not your place to make judgements against her. What has happened is between my sister and Ruggero. They should be encouraged · to get together and sort out their differences.'

'*Differences*, you call them?' Angelo emphasised the word with irony. 'You mean that Ruggero should be encouraged to pardon her infidelity?'

Terri shot a quick glance across at Vicki. Here was her perfect cue to launch in with her case of repentance. But Vicki didn't utter a sound. She was staring at the floor as though transfixed.

Terri looked back at Angelo. 'You once said yourself, I seem to remember, that it wasn't your business. Perhaps you've forgotten that?'

He shook his head. 'I have not forgotten. And, as far as I am aware, I have not made it my business. It appears to me that you are the one who is most anxious to interfere.'

Terri bit her lip. 'Only because I want to see fair

play. As the outsider, my sister is at a disadvantage. She needs someone to stand up for her when the whole Montefalcone clan is ganging up against her.'

He threw her a scathing smile. 'I see no one ganging up. I see only a faithless wife paying the price of her infidelity.'

'Isn't the loss of her child rather a high price?'

'It is not I who have set the price, *cara* Teresa.' He held her eyes. 'But, since you ask my opinion, I have to confess that my heart does not exactly bleed with sympathy.'

She glared across the desk at him, faintly chilled by the ruthlessness in his eyes. 'What heart?' she demanded sarcastically.

But he cut through the remark. 'She should have thought about her child before she jumped into bed with that——'

'You see? I told you!' With an angry cry, Vicki jumped to her feet. Her face was pale as she turned to Terri and tears of frustration glittered in her eyes. 'I told you it was a waste of time coming to see him. He hates me! He won't do anything to help!' She swung away impetuously. 'I'm not staying around to be insulted by him. I've had all I need of that!' A moment later she was heading for the door.

'Vicki, come back!' Terri felt her heart sink as she watched her sister flounce away. This was the worst thing she could have done. Behaving like a petulant child was scarcely likely to bring Angelo round. As the door slammed, she started to go after her. 'Wait,

Vicki!' But she got no farther than a couple of steps.

'Leave her.' Suddenly Angelo was on his feet, half leaning across the desk. His face was like thunder, his voice a command. 'Let her go!' he warned.

Automatically, Terri hesitated, seeming to hover in mid-air.

'If she wants to play the spoiled brat, then let her. I have no time for her childish games.' He straightened slowly and moved round to the front of the desk. He narrowed his eyes as he looked at her. 'I think, Teresa, you have all the proof you need of your sister's immaturity.'

She glared at him accusingly. 'You pushed her! Why did you have to? She was already upset enough.'

With an impatient gesture he leaned against the desk. 'Stop being her nursemaid, Teresa. Let her learn to stand on her own two feet.'

'You can be so damned callous!'

'You think so?' An amused smile curled the corners of his lips. 'I would call it being realistic. Facing the truth.'

'I suppose you would!'

'Why don't you try it some time?' He raised an enquiring eyebrow at her. 'Or do you intend to spend the rest of your life running behind your little sister and clearing up every mess she makes?'

'If I want to!' She met the coolly dissecting gaze with a show of defiance. 'And I certainly don't have to ask *your* permission one way or the other. You may run everybody else's life around here, but you don't run mine!'

Angelo regarded her for a moment, thoughtfully. 'Does she rush to comfort you when you're in trouble?' he enquired.

Terri frowned at him, suddenly completely halted in her tracks. It had never even crossed her mind that Vicki might do such a thing. 'Of course not,' she answered. 'I wouldn't expect her to.'

'So who *do* you turn to, Teresa, when you need a bit of sympathy? You've told me yourself there have been such times.'

She threw him a resentful look. The slightly barren truth was that, apart from her mother during her childhood, there had never really been anyone. Defensively, she shot back at him, 'I don't need someone to mop up my tears. Maybe I'm like you—totally self-sufficient.'

He smiled. 'You flatter me.'

'I promise you that wasn't my intention.'

He continued to stand there, leaning against the desk, watching her with those all-seeing eyes. 'So is it true? Are you really?' he asked.

In growing alarm, she fended him off. 'Am I really what?' she asked.

'Totally self-sufficient?'

'I like to think so.'

'Ah, Teresa, *mia cara*.' Angelo shook his head and straightened slightly. 'For such an attractive female as yourself, I think that would be a terrible waste.'

She knew he was going to move towards her and she wanted to move away. To escape out of reach of the sudden indefinable threat he seemed to pose. But she felt rooted to the spot, like a rabbit caught in headlights—perversely drawn. One small movement, she thought in fear-stricken folly, and I could fall right into his arms.

It was at that very moment that Vicki chose to make her entrance. She glanced at her sister and then at Angelo. 'I've come back to apologise,' she said.

Terri's heart was clamouring like a bell inside her chest. She had just been saved from something by the skin of her teeth—and she was neither certain from what nor if she had even wanted to be saved. Still scrambling mentally for composure, she watched as Angelo turned away and responded sharply over his shoulder, 'You could have saved yourself the bother. Really, there's no need.'

'Oh, but there is.' There was an unaccustomed firmness in Vicki's voice as she walked, straight-backed, across the room to stand directly in front of him. Her head was held high. 'Terri brought me here so that I could explain—and that's precisely what I'm going to do.'

As Angelo looked about to cut her short, she hurried on determinedly, 'I've made a terrible mistake. I acted foolishly and I'm deeply sorry that I did. I don't think I realised the seriousness of what I was doing until it was too late.'

'Vicki . . .' On a sudden protective urge, Terri interrupted her. But with a wave of her hand, Vicki silenced her.

'Neither of you may actually believe this,' she went

on, 'but I've grown up a lot in the past week or so. The fear that I might lose my baby gave me the biggest shock of my life. And the fear of losing Ruggero too. I love them. They're my life.' A sudden tremor in the steady voice. 'I know as surely as I'm standing here that if I'm given a second chance I would never do anything again that would jeopardise my family in any way.'

Her eyes held Angelo's levelly. 'I know you've always thought of me as an immature and spoiled brat—and maybe, to some extent, you were right. But I've changed, I swear I have. If I'm given the chance, I'll prove it to you.' She took a deep breath. 'All I'm asking is that you help me find Ruggero so that I can sort things out with him.'

As she came to the end of her dignified entreaty, a silence fell across the room. Terri held her breath, her gaze shifting from her sister's drawn face to fix expectantly on Angelo. Surely, she was praying to herself, even he must have been moved by Vicki's plea.

An interminable moment followed. Angelo's eyes were fixed on Vicki, an unfathomable expression on his face. Then, abruptly, he turned away and crossed to the chair behind his desk. As he sat down he said at last in a firm, quiet voice, 'Very well, I shall contact Ruggero.' He flicked a glance across at Terri. 'I had news this morning of where he is.' Then he directed his gaze at Vicki again. 'I shall request him to return immediately to the island. What happens after that is up to you.'

A warm flood of gratitude swept through Terri. She crossed to Vicki and slipped an arm round her shoulder as the younger girl's composure slipped just a fraction and an emotional tear rolled down her face. Then she glanced across at Angelo. 'Thank you,' she said.

'Don't thank me.' He was watching the scene with a wry, detached eye. 'The solution to this affair lies in the hands of your sister and my cousin, not in mine.' He allowed a significant pause before adding, 'Nor in yours, *mia cara* Teresa. You can relax now. There is no more that you can do.'

'Yes.' She nodded. Her job was done.

The dark eyes were still on her face. He smiled faintly. 'So, your journey was not wasted, after all.' He paused. 'You can go back to England now knowing that you have achieved your aims.'

Terri looked back at him, feeling the cold finality of his words. Once more he was inviting her to leave—and she had no more excuses to remain. She watched as his eyes shifted back to Vicki and vaguely heard him say, 'Now I would suggest that you go back home and wait there until I have news for you.'

Vicki nodded. 'I'll be waiting.' Then, with a swift glance across at Terri, she started to move towards the door.

With an oddly bereft feeling, Terri followed her. She didn't even dare to glance at the figure still seated behind the desk. 'Goodbye,' she murmured under her breath.

She was half-way through the door when he called

her back. She spun round with a sudden reckless lift in her heart to see that he was smiling at her. 'Perhaps,' he was saying, 'if you're not averse to taking an evening off from your nursemaid duties, you wouldn't mind joining me for dinner tonight?'

As Terri stared back mutely at him, not certain if she'd heard him right, he added with a lift of one eyebrow, 'No handcuffs this time. You're perfectly free to refuse if you wish.'

But she had no wish to refuse. Stupidly, she nodded. 'That would be nice.'

'Till later, then. I look forward to it. I'll send a car for you about eight o'clock.'

Terri was half-way to the lift before she allowed herself to smile. And half-way across the courtyard, with Vicki hurrying ahead of her towards the waiting car, before she dared to admit to herself that something very strange was happening to her heart.

It was flying, like a falcon, heading for the sun.

CHAPTER SEVEN

'WELL, fancy that!'

They were back at Vicki's villa after the interview, and Terri had just confessed to her sister why she wouldn't be free for dinner that night. 'It was quite out of the blue,' she protested innocently—and inwardly steeled herself for the onslaught to come.

But Vicki just shrugged tiredly. 'Well, you'll be better off having dinner with him tonight than you would have been with me. After all that drama, I'm totally whacked!'

'But at least we got what we wanted.' Terri smiled reassuringly at the weary figure on the sofa—and hastily steered the conversation away from her impending dinner date with Angelo. For the moment, that was not something she wished to discuss. She hadn't even sorted out her own feelings about it yet.

Vicki sighed and threw her a grateful glance. 'It all worked out, thanks to you,' she said.

'It was you who convinced him.' And it was true. Back there at the Casa Grande, Vicki had demonstrated a side to herself that Terri had never seen before. She told her now with pride and conviction, 'You're going to be OK, Vicki. Everything's going to turn out right.'

'I hope so.'

'You'll see.' Terri smiled kindly and started to stand up. 'I'll leave you now, you look exhausted. Take my advice and go off to bed for a couple of hours.'

'I think I will.' Vicki stifled a yawn. 'I've hardly slept at all over the past few days.' Then she blinked at Terri. 'Are you sure you don't mind going back to stay at the beach villa on your own?'

'Of course not.' She smiled. 'You don't want me here in the way when Ruggero gets back, do you?' Then she added with a faint pang of regret, 'Besides, I won't be staying much longer. There's nothing to keep me now.'

Vicki frowned. 'But you promise you'll stay till Ruggero arrives?'

'I already said I would!' Terri chided. 'Stop worrying.' She bent to kiss her sister on the cheek. 'You get some rest. I'll call you tomorrow. From the look of you, you'll sleep round the clock!'

Terri spent the rest of the day swimming, lying in the sun and trying to convince herself there was no earthly reason why she should be feeling so excited about tonight. Angelo had meant nothing by the invitation. The invitation meant nothing to her. This frantic scurrying inside her breast every time she thought ahead to eight o'clock was pure, unadulterated folly. It was time she got a grip on herself.

She tried on two outfits before finally plumping for the white—a simple button-front cotton sundress that, dressed up with a striking silver necklace and matching earrings, managed to look surprisingly chic.

She tied her hair up on top of her head. Then she took it down again. Tonight, she decided, she would leave it loose, falling to her shoulders in a curtain of pale silk, free and unrestrained.

She doused herself with Shalimar and glanced at her watch for the thousandth time, retouched her lipstick, checked the time again, and was just giving her reflection a last look-over when she heard car tyres on the gravel outside.

Relief and a sharp excitement surged through her. At last she was on her way.

A big moon hung on the horizon. Terri watched as it dipped and vanished, then magically reappeared again, as they made their way along the palm-lined cliff road that wound its way to the Casa Grande. Then they were sweeping into the courtyard where the fountain played, its dancing waters like liquid crystal against the floodlit sandstone walls.

As the chauffeur came round to open her door, she caught the chorus of cicadas on the still night air. And she sighed as, like a gossamer mantle, the warmth of the evening stole round her shoulders as she stepped out from the cool interior of the car on to the moonlit cobbles. She breathed in deeply, savouring the soft, scented air, and began to walk towards the big, carved door. A pulse of nervous anticipation was beating in her breast.

'*Buona sera*, Teresa.'

Out of the shadow of the colonnades stepped a tall,

elegant figure in a slim, dark suit, hair like midnight, a smile of welcome on his lips.

Terri started—and not simply because he had taken her by surprise. At the sight of him, her heart had flown to her throat. She could feel it fluttering there now, like a helpless, captive bird. She swallowed and stepped forward. '*Buona sera*, Angelo,' she replied.

'You're looking very lovely tonight.' He seemed to pause just for a moment, then he came towards her and kissed her on each cheek.

It was a perfectly ordinary, mundane greeting, the norm between acquaintances in this part of the world. But the light brush of his lips, the fleeting pressure of his hand on her arm, sent a charge of electricity through her veins. 'Thank you,' she only just managed to croak. It was the first time that Angelo had greeted her this way.

He led her indoors, then up in the lift to the very top floor, through an archway and down a corridor to a set of double carved doors at the end. 'Please, Teresa,' he invited as he stood aside to let her pass ahead of him into the room beyond. Then, as he came alongside her again, 'Would you care for a drink? What will you have?'

She allowed herself a brief glance round the room before answering, sensing that this was a part of the old fortress to which only a very few were granted access. The falcon's inner sanctum. And it was perfectly exquisite.

The room was as big as a polo pitch, furnished with the ubiquitous brocade-covered divans piled with jewel-coloured, shimmering silk cushions. Heavy, low coffee-tables were ranged around the edge of a vast Persian rug and discreet, hidden lights illuminated the breathtaking set of murals that decorated the walls.

A man in a blue and black uniform hovered in a corner, semi-invisible, as Terri answered, 'I'd like one of those aperitifs I had before.'

And Angelo translated, '*Due amari.*'

The man moved smoothly and instantly into action, taking glasses and a bottle from a dark carved cabinet and pouring two generous measures.

At Angelo's invitation, she sank down on one of the divans and glanced admiringly round the room once more. 'It's beautiful,' she told him, unable to keep the compliment to herself. And she was glad she had said it, for he looked pleased.

'I'm glad you like it.' He sat down opposite her with a smile as the man in the blue and black uniform appeared before her with their drinks on a tray.

'Thank you.' She helped herself, then waited till Angelo had his.

'*Salute*! To your health!' He raised his glass to her as the servant melted off into the shadows again.

She responded, '*Salute*!'

And he added in a careful tone, 'This evening I have only one request to make of you. We can talk about any subject you wish, any subject under the sun—but, just for a change, let's keep off the subject of your sister.'

Terri made a face. 'Very well,' she agreed. Then she

added hastily, before he could cut in, 'But not until I've thanked you properly for your promise to help her this morning. We're both extremely grateful to you.'

He shrugged and narrowed his eyes at her. 'All I promised was to bring Ruggero back to the island. What happens after that is not up to me.'

'I know.' She nodded. 'But it's a start. I think Vicki will be able to handle the rest.'

Angelo took a mouthful of the bitter, dark liquid and eyed her over the rim of his glass. 'Perhaps,' he agreed. 'Perhaps she really has learned her lesson—and grown up in the process, as she claims.'

Terri allowed herself a slight smile as he held her eyes. On his part, this was quite a turnaround. And perhaps he was able to read her mind, for he went on, laying his glass aside, 'No doubt my attitude at the start struck you as a little harsh. I may have appeared too quick to condemn. After all,' he consented with a light smile, 'we all make mistakes from time to time.' But, lest she misjudge the scope of this sudden display of lenience, he quickly added the unequivocal rider, 'It is well, however, for your sister—and for her illicit lover—that she is not married to me. Peccadilloes of that nature are not among those I would tolerate in a wife.' He held her eyes for a moment lest she doubt it, then relaxed his gaze and leaned back in his seat. 'My cousin, however, is of a less demanding temperament. He may well find it in his heart to forgive this passing indiscretion.' He raised a dark eyebrow at her. 'Though I have to say I never would.'

Terri had no difficulty at all in believing that. And though her own views on marital fidelity were similarly stringent, she couldn't resist a little dig. 'I wonder how you would cope if you were married to an equally unforgiving woman?'

A flicker of amusement crossed his face. 'I seem to remember you making reference to my supposed double standards once before. But let me assure you that I am not in the habit of applying standards to others that I do not also expect from myself.' He held her eyes. 'When I finally find the woman for me, she may be assured I will not stray.'

He paused for a moment, then smiled, adding half seriously, 'Perhaps that is another reason why I am not married yet. I am not quite ready for such restrictions.' Then he leaned towards her and changed the subject. 'I'm going to have another drop of *amaro*. How about you?' he asked.

Terri drank from her glass and shook her head. 'No, thanks—I'm fine.' Then she watched through lowered lashes as he signalled to the man in the corner and the man came soundlessly across the carpet to top up the dark liquid in his glass. As the man moved away again, she asked, following Angelo's lead away from personal matters, 'Tell me about the Casa Grande. How old is it? How long has it been in your family?'

'For centuries.' He leaned back, resting his head against the deep red cushions, surveying her through long, dark lashes. 'Though it has passed through many and varied hands in the course of its history.

Greek, Roman, Arab, Ottoman—we've been occupied by all of them.' The well-shaped mouth curved into a smile. 'Like most Sicilians, I carry in my veins a little of the blood of each of them.'

How very romantic, Terri thought. Her own background seemed dull by comparison. She pulled a face. 'I'm afraid the most exotic connection I can lay claim to is an Irish grandmother on my father's side.'

Angelo smiled. 'So that's where that streak of impetuosity comes from?'

She glanced away, not certain whether he was poking fun. 'What streak of impetuosity?' she wanted to know.

He drained his drink. 'Oh, it's there all right. What else brought you flying half-way across Europe at the drop of a hat? In spite of everything——' he laid down his glass '—I couldn't help admiring you for that.'

Abruptly, Terri lowered her eyes.

'You seem surprised.' There was gentle amusement in his voice.

Terri shook her head. Surprise was only one of the emotions she felt as she fought back the faint blush in her cheeks and struggled to meet the dark gaze again. She felt flattered, delighted and confused—and more than mildly irritated at herself that she should feel anything at all. How could she possibly allow such a throwaway compliment to turn her head?

With disciplined detachment, she answered calmly, 'I don't think it was an exceptional thing to do. Vicki's my sister, after all.'

'But not every sister would have done it.' Then,

with a wry smile, he held up his hand. 'But we're getting into dangerous waters. This is the one subject we agreed to keep off.'

It was at that moment that a man in waiter's uniform appeared through the double doors. He made a brief signal to Angelo, who inclined his head momentarily to acknowledge it. He turned to Terri. 'Dinner will be ready in a moment. Unless you'd like another *amaro*, we can go through now.'

She drained her glass. 'No, that's fine by me.' Then, following his example, she rose to her feet.

He told her, 'I've asked for dinner to be served on the terrace. I hope that's all right with you?'

'Sounds nice.' Smoothing the skirt of her slim white dress, she followed him across the room to the open french doors on the other side. Then she stopped in her tracks and gasped in wonder at the sight that met her eyes. Perhaps 'nice' had been a bit of an understatement!

The terrace was almost as big as the room they had just left—circular in shape, bounded by a waist-high iron railing and jutting out over the edge of the cliff with a spectacular view across the bay. Beneath a cloudless, starlit sky, the lights of the marina twinkled and danced while, further out, she caught the bright, intermittent flash of the lazily bobbing marker buoys. And beyond those, on the still horizon, the low-hanging, luminescent moon.

She crossed to the railing and leaned against it. 'It's like a fairyland!' she breathed.

Angelo had come to stand a few paces behind. 'On a

clear autumn day you can see Tunisia from here.
We're closer to the coast of Africa than we are to
mainland Italy.'

'Really?' A ripple of excitement went through her at
the thought. Africa. The Dark Continent. Somehow,
the very name summoned up images of adventure,
mystery and intrigue. She turned to the dark-suited
figure at her back and felt a strange, overpowering
sensation as she looked up into his face. As though
some indefinable power in him were drawing
her—and she, helpless, half willing and vulnerable,
had no option but to surrender. 'I had no idea,' she
told him, half mesmerised by the witchcraft in his
eyes, 'that your island was such an enchanted place.'

As he reached out to touch her arm, she felt a shiver
rush across her skin. Then, as his fingers clasped her
naked flesh, there was a sudden, sharp tightening in
her breast. But he only smiled. 'Come, Teresa,' he
said. 'I'll tell you more about the island while we
eat.'

He led her a little way further along the terrace to
where a table was laid for two and a waiter was already
standing by, uncorking a bottle of wine. Beneath the
soft lights that shone from the fortress walls the
damask cloth, fine crystal and heavy silver cutlery
gleamed richly. He pulled back a chair for her and she
sat, feeling suddenly overwhelmed by it all. By the
beauty, the magnificence, the sheer perfection of her
surroundings—and not least, she secretly confessed to
herself, by the presence of the man.

As he seated himself opposite her now, Terri

glanced across at him and felt again the magnetic power, the potent magic he wrought on her. No harm, she told herself. There was no reason why tonight she could not simply allow herself to enjoy the company of a virile, attractive man. After all, it had been so long. And besides, this uncanny effect he was having on her was simply the moonlight and the night. The spell would wear off in the cold light of day. She was in no danger. No danger at all.

They were served Persian melon with *prosciutto* to start. The sweet succulence of the honeydewed fruit blended exquisitely with the sharp, salty tang of the Parma ham. Terri ate with appetite and sipped appreciatively at the light red wine. 'A local wine?' she ventured, smiling, laying down her glass.

Angelo smiled back at her. 'Of course. Self-sufficiency is our aim, as you know.' Then he went on, deliberately holding her eyes, 'It is a young wine, not too full-bodied, a wine that has not yet reached its peak.' He paused to drink, letting his eyes drift unhurriedly over the wide scoop neckline, the bare, tanned shoulders, the small high breasts beneath the cotton of her dress. 'With careful handling it promises to mature well.'

Terri swallowed awkwardly, her flesh burning beneath that sensual gaze, the probing, sexually explicit eyes. She said crassly, 'I'm afraid I don't know the first thing about wine.'

'Wines are like women.' He held her eyes. 'Each with its own particular qualities—its particular flavour, its particular style. Though many are quite unremarkable, even disappointing to the connoisseur, there are always that special few that make one's indulgence well worth while.'

His indulgence—in women—was something she had already guessed at, and he had more or less admitted it earlier. That he would also be a connoisseur, an expert, in such matters somehow went without saying. As she dropped her eyes from his face, they strayed to the long-fingered, well-shaped hands. And, quite recklessly, she found herself wondering what it would be like to be touched by those hands. *Really* touched. Then instantly she recoiled from the thought and snapped her eyes up as he went on, 'One of the most important considerations with any young wine is learning to judge when it is ready to be released. It must be kept in the vats until just the right time. If it is released too soon, it will be spoiled.' He reached for the wine bottle, causing a sudden panic in her heart, as though she believed he might be reaching for her. Yet it was relief tinged with a vague hint of anticlimax that she felt as he lifted the bottle from the white tablecloth and inclined it towards her glass with a smile. 'Timing, Teresa, is the crucial factor—in wine-making, as in everything else.'

With a demonstration of exquisite timing, the waiter reappeared. As he cleared away their plates and brought a platter of steamed fish, Terri eyed with discretion the composed dark features of the man seated opposite her. As once before, she had the feeling of having been brought to the brink of something—and, as then, was not quite certain now how pleased she really was to have been allowed to step back away from it in time.

As the meal progressed, the sudden electricity in the air between them seemed to subside a little, though it never completely disappeared. Terri could sense it, like a disconcerting buzz of excitement across the apparent normality, as they chatted away with remarkable ease about all sorts of things.

Over the veal and giant mushrooms, Angelo told her about his childhood on the island. 'Growing up in a place like this was something special,' he confessed. 'Especially with so many brothers and sisters and cousins to share it with.'

Over the cheeseboard, she told him about her own childhood. 'Potters Bar, north London, wasn't exactly Santa Pietrina, but we had a pretty good childhood. At least, until my father died.' She skirted the unhappy subject with an almost apologetic smile. 'That was when I had to grow up. My mother just sort of caved in for a while and left everything, more or less, in my hands.'

'That must have been hard.'

She shrugged. 'It wasn't so bad. I quite enjoyed looking after Vicki in a way. Besides,' she went on hurriedly, not wishing to dwell on a subject that was taboo, 'I've always found it easy to escape. I'm a terrible dreamer,' she confessed, aware that she was baring secrets she usually kept to herself. 'I used to invent my own little world—based on stories I'd read or films I'd seen. My imagination used to run wild!'

She paused, suddenly embarrassed by the rapt

expression on Angelo's face. 'I suppose all youngsters do that,' she defended herself. 'You must have done it yourself.'

He smiled sympathetically and told her, 'During my youth, this island was inhabited by more spacemen and little green monsters than any spaceship from Mars!'

It was later, as Terri laid down her spoon after devouring a delicious water ice, that he dropped his napkin on to the table and suddenly started to get to his feet. 'Let me show you something.' He smiled.

She regarded him with curiosity. 'What?' she wanted to know. Then she rose too, intrigued, as he came round the table to stand behind her and started to pull her chair away.

'Come.' He held out his hand to her. 'An old romantic like you should appreciate this,' he assured her.

He led her to the far side of the terrace, where the lights from the old fortress walls almost didn't reach—but she could pick out, below them, the rugged outline of the cliffs.

Angelo began, 'The very spot where we're standing is said to have been the scene of one of the most romantic stories they tell about the Casa Grande. Dates are a bit vague, but it was supposed to have been somewhere in the middle of the fifteenth century that the daughter of the prince who owned the Casa Grande at the time fell in love with an island boy, an apprentice falconer who worked for the prince——'

As he leaned with his back against the railings, his

features were caught in the light. Terri watched him and cut in, 'I suppose the prince didn't approve?'

He laughed. 'I'm afraid he did more than just disapprove. He took the young man in question—Arnaldo was his name—and threw him into the dungeon. The prince's daughter, Ismelda, was locked under guard in her room.'

Terri frowned. 'What happened next?'

She caught a twinkle in his eye as he followed the expression on her face. 'What happened next was that poor Ismelda pined away—but Arnaldo was determined to make her his bride. Using the buckle of his belt, he somehow managed to pick the lock of the dungeon door. Then, with the help of some friends, he disguised himself as a washerwoman and tricked his way into Ismelda's room. With Ismelda hidden in a basket of laundry, the two of them escaped out on to the balcony which used to be where we're standing now.'

'And got away?' Terri was all at once acutely anxious for the story to end well.

But Angelo slowly shook his head. 'He was just about to lower the basket over the side of the balcony on to the beach below when one of the prince's guard was alerted and rushed out on to the balcony brandishing a spear.'

'He didn't kill them, did he?' She felt faintly dejected at the thought.

But Angelo shook his head again. He smiled. 'At the very last moment, out of the sky, a splendid falcon appeared. He flew at the guard, knocking the spear

from his hand down on to the cliffs below, and gave
Arnaldo and Ismelda their chance to escape.' He
exchanged a smile with her. 'Much later, after the pair
were married and had sons and daughters of their
own, the old prince finally forgave them and allowed
them to return to the island. Arnaldo was made the
first Marchese de Montefalcone, and when the old
prince died, leaving no heir but his daughter, the
Marchese inherited the Casa Grande, and his heirs
have lived here ever since.'

'What a lovely story!'

He turned to gaze down over the railings. 'The tiny
cove where a boat was waiting to take the young
lovers to safety is down there, directly below us. And
behind the cove is a promontory of the cliff that looks
exactly like a falcon's head. In honour, so the legend
says, of the falcon who saved the young falconer's
life.'

Terri leaned alongside him with searching eyes,
scanning the side of the cliff. 'Where? Where is the
falcon's head?' she asked.

'I'm afraid you can't see it from here. Only from the
cove.'

She turned to him. 'Then let's go down!'

He smiled. 'How? In a laundry basket?'

She caught the teasing look in his eye and smiled
back. Then she pleaded, 'There must be *some* way!'
Suddenly she desperately wanted to go.

The dark eyes watched her face for a moment, then
he told her, 'As a matter of fact, there is a way. Here.'
He propelled her towards a half-hidden door set in the

thick stone wall. Then he pulled the door open and switched on a light to reveal a twisting staircase leading down. 'This leads directly into the cove. If you want to see the falcon, follow me.'

Their footsteps echoed softly as, in single file, they made their way down the rock-hewn stairs. Then, at the foot, another door led out on to the moonlit sand.

Angelo held out his hand to assist her as she stepped over the threshold, feeling the soft sand warm on her feet as she kicked off her sandals. She looked round her. The cove was tiny, little more than ten metres wide, bounded on three sides by the craggy cliff face, on the fourth by the gently lapping tide. She smiled. 'It feels like a secret place.'

'It is.' He led her along the sand. 'My brothers and sisters and I used to come swimming here when we were kids. Only immediate family were allowed.'

'So I should feel privileged?' she teased.

'Of course.' They had stopped beneath a jutting overhang and he was smiling as he guided her round to face the opposite side of the cove. 'There,' he said, pointing, directing her gaze to the rocks above. 'There's your falcon, Teresa.'

It took her just a minute to spot it, then there it was, as clear as day. The head and shoulders of a magnificent falcon, just like the ones she had seen at the farm. 'It looks almost as though it was carved by some sculptor from the rock!' she exclaimed.

'But it wasn't. It was formed by natural erosion over the years. And the only spot you can see it from is the spot where we're standing now. They say this is where the boat was hidden that was waiting to take the lovers away.'

She turned to him. 'It's such a beautiful story. Do you think it might be true?'

'Who knows? It might be.'

'I think there has to be some truth in it. It's too nice a story to be a lie.'

Angelo smiled, watching her. 'You really mean that, don't you?' Then, almost imperceptibly, he moved towards her.

She nodded, 'Of course,' aware of a strange look in his eyes. Then, abruptly, she dropped her gaze, seeming to freeze immobile to the spot as he reached out quite suddenly to touch her cheek with his fingertips.

'*Sei un dolce tesoro*,' he murmured.

Terri swallowed and glanced up again, hearing an unfamiliar note in his voice—somehow ragged yet unutterably tender. 'What does that mean?' she asked foolishly.

For an interminable moment he didn't answer, just continued to watch her with those fathomless black eyes. Then the hand on her cheek slipped lightly round to the back of her neck, smoothing her hair away from her face, sending tingles across her scalp. She held her breath, feeling her heart rush in her chest, aware of an incredible, deafening silence singing in her ears as, for a moment, he seemed to stand poised over her. Then he bent towards her. 'It means this,' he said.

The lips that came down to cover hers were soft and gentle, firm and warm. Expert, achingly erotic, sending her senses up in flames. She had no strength to resist him, no desire. As his free hand moved to circle her waist, drawing her nerveless body against his, she could feel the hard male strength of the broad chest crushing against her breasts, the urgent pressure of the long, lean thighs.

'Teresa, Teresa . . .' His hand swept across her shoulders, then slowly traced the length of her spine, making her tremble and shiver against him, weak and helpless in the power of his embrace.

Yet, somehow, her arms found the strength to slip around his shoulders, loving the strong, hard feel of them. And, almost of their own volition, her fingers caressed the silky-smooth hair at the nape of his neck. Then she felt the breath leave her body again as his mouth moved down to cover hers once more.

This kiss was not as gentle as the first. There was an urgency in it, a bolder, less subtle eroticism. As he prised her lips apart and invaded her warm, moist mouth with his tongue, she felt the blood leap in her veins and a clamour of excitement awaken deep down.

Her senses were swimming as his hand slipped round now to caress the mound of her breast, the strong hand firmly, yet softly, moulding the sensitive sphere through the fabric of her dress. Then she sighed as she felt him undo the buttons at the top, and a shaft of sheer carnal pleasure shot through her as his fingers made contact with her naked flesh.

It was exquisite—a bright, sharp, shimmering sensation, sweeter than anything she had ever known. As the palm of his hand brushed languorously over the hardening peak of her breast, she was overcome by a sudden deep longing more powerful than anything she could ever have dreamed.

With a low moan, she allowed him to draw her down softly on to the bed of sand, feeling the pulse in her throat throb violently as he quickly shed his jacket and tie. Then he was bending over her again, dropping kisses around her hairline, at the back of her ears, on the curve of her throat. Murmuring, 'Teresa, *tesoro*,' one arm holding her while his free hand, without haste, undid the remaining buttons of her dress . . .

She was totally naked beneath the dress except for a pair of tiny, lacy briefs. As the last of the buttons came free and the two halves of her sundress parted company to reveal her slim, lithe, lightly tanned body, she felt the dark eyes sweep over her. But she felt no embarrassment, no shame as on that first occasion when he had caught her topless on the beach. Just a sense of exaltation as he half smiled and bent to kiss her on the lips; a sense of celebration in her nakedness as he helped her to slip free of the dress.

But her own near-nakedness was not enough. With eager, unabashed fingers, she assisted as he began to undo the front of his shirt, letting her hand trail with delight over the hard male contours of his chest as he finally shrugged the loose garment away. Then she was stretching up to caress his shoulders and bury her face against the sun-darkened, hair-roughened warmth of the broad chest as he turned his attention to divesting himself, with equal rapidity, of his trousers.

A moment later he was astride her, his two hands cupping her uptilted breasts. With a sense of growing wonder at her own temerity, Terri reached out to glide her hand across the hard nubs of his nipples, the flat planes of his stomach—then swept down to caress the tautly muscled thighs, so dark against the light colour of his shorts.

'Teresa, *mia dolce* Teresa!' His fingers were working their magic on the thrusting, throbbing peaks of her breasts, squeezing between thumb and forefinger till she threw back her head and cried out with desire. Then he was down on her, the weight of him pressing against her thighs, his warm mouth closing over one swollen, excited aureole, biting, tugging, driving her wild.

'Angelo!' It was a cry released from her innermost being. As he pulled himself up to press his hungry, moist mouth against hers, his hands stroking her heated, eager flesh, sweeping between her shivering thighs, she was silently calling out to him, Now! Please take me now! Please, Angelo. The time is right!

But he did not. Though she could feel the excited beat of his heart still pounding against her own, by an almost tangible effort of will his hands and his lips grew still again. With a sigh that spoke of all the sharp frustration that this abrupt retreat was costing him, he slumped against her for a moment, then slowly began to raise himself up.

With a vague glaze of disappointment, Terri watched as he got to his feet, then reached out a hand to her, inviting her to do the same. 'Come, Teresa,' he said. 'Right now, I think the sea is the safest place.'

She followed him down to the edge of the water and watched as he ran the last few metres, then dived into the soft-rolling waves. As the dark head disappeared from sight, she held her breath for a moment and paused to examine the tumult in her breast. Something had happened to her—something profound, irreversible. Though it was not what she had thought might happen. Not what she had been expecting at all.

With a soft splash, Angelo reappeared, farther out now, well beyond her reach, and with slow, easy strokes began to swim. With dawning enlightenment, she stood and watched, then raised her eyes to the big silver moon.

Oh, lord, she thought. I love this man.

CHAPTER EIGHT

TERRI was still standing by the water's edge when Angelo turned round and began to swim back to the shore again. As he rose from the sea, his muscular, tanned body glistening with droplets silvered by the moon, she felt her heart contract in her chest. He was so splendid. And not just physically—in every way. An utterly worthy, if cruelly ill-selected, focus for her fledgling love.

As he came towards her, he was totally unaware of the upheaval he had wrought in her. He shook himself and pushed his fingers through the glistening black hair. 'I reckon a dip in the sea is the next best thing to a cold shower,' he told her with a faintly self-mocking grin. Then he added, 'We'd better be getting back now. I think it's time I took you home.'

She nodded, hiding the crush of disappointment—was he so abruptly to be wrenched away from her?—and followed his tall frame silently as he led her back across the sand. Their clothes lay scattered like blown leaves after a windstorm, testimony to the brief, blissful madness that had overtaken them. Terri watched from the corner of her eye as, with unhurried speed, he pulled on his trousers and shirt—and had a strange, sad sense of something being taken away from her. Placed out of bounds. She shook the thought away.

She was buttoning the last button on her dress when, all at once, he was standing before her. As she glanced up, her heart standing still, he smiled. 'Teresa, *tesoro*,' he murmured, and for a long, giddy moment looked into her eyes.

Then, ever so gently, he drew her into his arms and held her, warm and safe, against his chest. As his hand lightly caressed her hair, she resisted the urge to cling to him and pour out all the tortured emotions that were raging in her heart. He would not understand. He would not even wish to know.

With a sigh he released her and bent to plant a brief, chaste kiss on her forehead. He took her hand. 'Come, Teresa, let's go,' he said.

They met no one on their journey through the drawing-room, then down in the lift. No discreetly lurking blue and black uniforms. Outside, he led her to a far corner of the courtyard where the red Ferrari was parked, and held the door open while she climbed inside.

Then they were heading along the cliff road, away from the Casa Grande towards the villa. Two figures in a moonlit landscape who both knew that nothing could be quite the same again.

There was no word from Angelo for two days after that.

Though Terri consoled herself that, eventually, he had to get in touch—if only with news of Laura and

Ruggero—she knew within herself that his silence boded ill. It was, she sensed, his way of telling her that those moments on the beach had been a mere lapse, a transitory, meaningless transgression of the flesh, simply to be forgotten and never thought of again.

Alas—if only, for her, that were possible! But she knew beyond a doubt that it was not. For her, what had passed between them had been no mere carnal lapse. Though an awakening of the senses, she could not deny, it had also been much more than that—an abrupt and reckless awakening of the heart.

It had taken her quite by surprise, but she had known as surely as if she had seen it written across the sky that she had fallen hopelessly in love with Angelo.

This uncanny revelation was not something that, right now, she could share with Vicki. The elation, the confusion, the fear in her soul were emotions best kept to herself. As a cover for her own personal anxieties, she reverted to her role as comforter as Vicki chafed at the lack of news.

'He'll be in touch soon,' she assured her with more equanimity than she felt. 'Didn't he say he would be?' she chided. If there was one thing certain in this world, she knew, it was that Angelo de Montefalcone was a man of his word. 'He promised to get Ruggero to come back, and I'm sure that's precisely what he's doing.'

'I know, I know.' Vicki hugged her apologetically. 'You're the last person I should be complaining to. You've already done so much for me.' She made a self-deprecating face. 'It's just that I can't help worrying.

I've made such a mess of things. All I want now is the chance to try and sort them out.'

'I'm sure you'll get it,' Terri promised her. 'Just be patient a little while longer.' But, though Vicki was still understandably anxious and upset, Terri could sense a definite change in their relationship. Vicki was no longer the dependent little girl running to her big sister to sort things out. There was a new poise in her demeanour, a new maturity.

It was ironic, Terri couldn't help thinking, that just as Vicki had decided to grow up she was the one who, for a change, felt in need of a little comfort and support.

Angelo finally called early on the third day. Terri was just emerging from the shower when Grazia called through to her, '*Telefono, signorina! È il Marchese Angelo!*'

With just a towel pulled hastily round her, Terri flew through to the bedroom and grabbed the extension to her ear. 'Hello?' Her heart was beating like a drum.

He was brief and distant, she acknowledged with a shiver to herself. 'I want you to phone your sister and tell her to be ready in a couple of hours. I'll be round for you in half an hour.'

And that was it. No explanations. No reassurances. Just a rather brusque set of instructions. Terri dried herself hurriedly. What on earth was going on? But her heart was dancing in spite of herself, just at the prospect of seeing him again. She pulled on a simple denim skirt and a white cotton top, and was already waiting out on the terrace when the red Ferrari came crunching down the drive.

'*Buon giorno.*' He climbed out, a tall, dark figure in body-hugging jeans and a loose white shirt with rolled-back sleeves. A fierce, raw pleasure went through her at the sight of him. After two days of darkness, the sun shone again. She grinned inanely as he pulled open the passenger door and stood aside—no greeting kiss this time, she noted—then instructed her baldly, 'Get in.'

She got in. Then, as Angelo climbed in beside her, she turned to him nervously. 'Where are we going? What's going on? Have you spoken to Ruggero? Has he come back yet?'

At the fusillade of questions his face broke into a smile. 'One at a time,' he chided her good-humouredly. Then he added mysteriously, 'Don't worry, all will be revealed soon enough. In the meantime, I have something to show you.'

'What?'

But he was giving nothing away. As the big car headed out on to the road, he turned to toss her a tantalising wink. 'A surprise,' he insisted. 'Patience, Teresa. Just wait and see.'

She was able to figure out one thing, at least, as they took to the narrow mountain road, soon leaving the sea stretched out below them like a vast azure pool. Unless she was very much mistaken, they were heading for the farm. But what could the surprise he had promised her be? As they turned in through the gates, she had a sudden inspiration. 'I think I know what you're going to show me,' she told him with an excited smile.

'Do you, indeed?' He grinned conspiratorially at her as they climbed out of the car and he started to lead her across the farm forecourt towards the falcons' mews. 'Come on, then. Let's see if you're right.'

She was. She felt her heart turn over with pleasure as Angelo led her to the little window and invited her to look inside. Last time, there had been a mother falcon brooding on her eggs. This time, the scene had been totally transformed. 'Oh, they're gorgeous!' Terri gasped at the sight of the four scrawny, half-naked chicks, all wide-open beaks and staggering claws as they huddled round their proud mother.

Entranced, she watched as the mother falcon tore pieces of raw meat from the chunk in her claws, then, with utmost delicacy, deposited a tiny portion into each upturned, gaping mouth. Terri turned to Angelo with a sense of awe. 'When were they born?' she wanted to know.

He smiled. 'They hatched yesterday. Amilcare phoned to tell me as soon as I got back last night.'

So he had been away. But she resisted the temptation to start quizzing him again. He had told her she would know soon enough what had transpired. Trying to force it out of him would only be a waste of time. Instead, she turned back with growing wonder to watch the little family scene. This was indeed the nicest surprise.

Angelo was watching her. He told her, 'I thought you'd want to see them before——' Then he stopped in mid-sentence and glanced away. 'I knew you'd want to see them,' he amended carefully.

Terri forced a controlled smile. 'You were right.' And she wondered what he had been about to say. Before you left? She felt a sharp, painful tug. Over the past forty-eight hours, she had almost forgotten that she would be leaving the island before very long. The only thought that had filled her mind had been the thought of seeing him again.

He leaned forward to look at the chicks. 'Pretty soon these scrawny little bags of bones will be transformed into four little balls of down. And from then on they'll just keep eating and growing until they've got their adult feathers.'

Terri was watching him, a sense of uneasiness growing inside her. All at once she was aware of a distance, a coolness, about his demeanour. She said nothing as, without glancing at her, he went on, 'In six weeks or so they'll be flying—and not long after that they'll be ready to go off on their own.'

'So soon?' It was a happy thought, but a sad one too. Terri glanced across at the mother bird. 'Won't she mind when they fly away?'

Angelo shrugged an indifferent shrug. 'Who knows? But that's the way it happens. When the time comes, they just fly away. Like me, the falcons hate goodbyes.' He turned now to regard her with detached, unsentimental eyes. 'In nature, as in life, bonds must be broken. That is the way of things. It is pointless to try and fight against it.'

Terri felt a sense of sharp rebuke at the blunt, chilly

message his words contained. And as she looked up into the cold, uncaring eyes, he was suddenly a million light-years away from the man who, just two nights ago, had come so close to making love to her. The man who had recounted with such warmth the legend of the thwarted lovers and taken her to see the falcon in the cliff. It was even hard to recognise in that closed, uncompromising face the man who had so spontaneously brought her here.

She dropped her eyes and asked him. 'The young falcons—do they ever return?'

Angelo shook his head. 'No, never, according to our records. Once they're gone, they're gone for good.' Almost impatiently, he glanced at his watch. 'It's time we were getting back on the road. We have to go and pick up your sister.'

Terri followed him back to the car with that dull, hollow sensation of one who has just been brought sharply back down to earth. Her brief flight of fantasy, he had made it very clear, had ended in a spectacular nosedive. Without even touching directly on the subject, he had managed to spell out in no uncertain terms that the other night down in the cove was all there was ever going to be. Their paths had briefly overlapped, but now they must go their separate ways.

She was surprised as, when they got back into the car, he paused after switching on the engine and took from the glove compartment a small, neat parcel, wrapped in tissue paper. He held it out to her. 'For you,' he said. Then he shifted swiftly into gear.

Terri unwrapped it slowly, aware that her fingers felt quite numb. Then she smiled as she saw what it contained—the purple leather hood with the pink and blue plumes that Khan, the father of the new-born baby chicks, had worn on their outing last time she was here.

'I saw you admiring it.' He adroitly turned the car around and headed back towards the road. 'I thought you might like to have it as a reminder of the falcons.'

So it was a goodbye gift. Her fingers tensed around it as she laid it in her lap. 'Thank you,' she told him stiffly, not daring to glance across at his face. If only he knew, she thought with a stab of bitterness, that she would need no reminder of the falcons—nor of any of what had befallen her over the past few days. Her experiences on Santa Pietrina were forged forever on her heart.

It seemed no time at all before they had left the mountain road and were heading back towards the villa. 'First we'll pick up your car,' Angelo explained, 'then we'll drive separately to your sister's place. From there, the two of you just follow me.'

Terri was still none the wiser as to their ultimate destination until shortly after they had picked up Vicki. Seated tensely in the passenger seat next to her as she kept her eyes glued to the red car in front, Vicki all at once sat forward and exclaimed, 'He's taking us to Donna Rosaria's! His mother's place!' She turned to Terri with an excited grin. 'I'll bet you anything that Laura and Ruggero are there!'

As they drew closer, Terri caught a glimpse,

between the trees, of a stately, white-walled villa. Then they were following Angelo through the gates and along a driveway to the front of the house, and she was manoeuvring the white Autobianchi into a space alongside the Ferrari.

Almost before she had pulled on the handbrake, Vicki was struggling with the door-handle. Then, breathlessly, she was careering after Angelo as, with a nod in their direction, he started to head towards the house. With a growing sense of sadness Terri watched them go. All at once she felt superfluous. There was no need for her to be here any more.

The front door of the villa was standing open and, as Terri approached, Vicki was already following Angelo across the hall. As she hurried after them, she could hear the sound of voices within. There was an almost tangible anticipation crackling in the air.

Quickly, heading in the direction of the voices, she made her way towards what appeared to be an elegantly furnished drawing-room. Then she crossed the threshold just in time to catch the moment of sheer magic that her trip to the island had been all about. A shaft of emotion went through her, bringing sharp tears to her eyes, as she watched Vicki's face light up with unrestrained relief and joy at the sight of the chubby, dark-haired toddler who was running, arms outstretched, towards her across the room.

'*Mamma*! *Mamma*!'

The next instant the little girl was in her mother's arms, her tiny tanned arms hugging her mother's neck, her tiny face beaming with delight.

'Oh, Laura, *tesoro*! It's so good to see you!' Vicki kissed her and ruffled her hair. 'I've missed you so much!'

The child gurgled happily, apparently oblivious to all the emotions that were flying round the room—but as Terri stole a brief glance at the grey-haired woman in the blue silk dress who was standing with Angelo to one side, she could tell she was not the only spectator in the room who had tears in her eyes.

With an excited gurgle, little Laura pulled free from her mother's embrace and darted to retrieve a floppy doll that had been abandoned on a nearby sofa. '*Mamma*—Luisa!' she announced, showing the doll proudly to her mother—evidently considering it her first priority that her mother should be introduced immediately to the latest addition to the family.

Terri watched the happy scene, smiling quietly to herself. One thing was perfectly obvious—during all the recent emotional traumas the child had been well and happy, and was quite evidently none the worse for her brief separation from her mother. Just as Angelo had assured her all along. She threw him a grateful sideways glance, then turned towards the slightly uncertain-looking figure in the light grey suit who had suddenly appeared in the doorway.

The grey-suited figure cleared his throat. 'Vicki?' he said.

There was a pause and an electric silence as Vicki turned to look at him. Then her eyes filled with tears and she bit her lip. 'Ruggero!' she breathed. A moment later the tension was broken as Ruggero stepped forward and swept her in his arms.

It was then that Angelo stepped out of the background and took the proceedings in hand. He glanced across at Terri as he spoke. 'I think you should know,' he said, 'that little Laura has been here with her grandmother all the time. Her father returned only this morning, but the child has never been off the island.'

Vicki gasped, 'But I——!'

And he added pointedly, 'You assumed that Ruggero had taken her away, but you were quite wrong.'

It was time now for Ruggero himself to have his say. He straightened his shoulders and narrowed his eyes as he directed himself to his wife. 'After our row I just wanted to get away—to be somewhere on my own, to have a chance to think. I had a business appointment in Genoa coming up, then another one in Hamburg, so I decided just to string them together and disappear for a while. I couldn't take Laura with me—that wouldn't have been fair on her—but I was scared that you might try to take her back to England while I was gone, and I couldn't bear the thought of losing her as well as you.'

As Vicki laid an apologetic hand on his sleeve, he went on, 'So I left her with her grandmother—and swore Mother and Angelo to secrecy.'

Terri glanced across at Angelo. He had kept the secret well—but suddenly she didn't blame him in the least. It had, after all, been in the interests of the child that she be kept in a secure and familiar environment till the storm that raged around her had finally blown itself out.

And it appeared as though it had. Ruggero slipped an arm around Vicki and told her solemnly, 'I realise I was partly to blame for what happened—and I hope I can put it right. Even if Angelo hadn't come flying all the way across to Germany to demand that I come straight back——' he allowed himself a fleeting, wry smile at that '—I'd already decided I'd stayed away quite long enough.'

As Vicki hugged him, Terri turned discreetly away and glanced across at Angelo. So that was where he had been for the past two days—over in Germany on a mission of mercy not dissimilar to her own! She felt a surge of gratitude—and something illogically akin to pride. Somehow, such a gesture was even more than she had expected of him.

As he caught her eye, he came towards her with a smile. 'I hope you will forgive my small deception regarding the whereabouts of the child?'

She smiled back at him without reserve. The deception had been one of omission, not commission, she now realised. Not once had Angelo ever said that Laura was with Ruggero. That was the conclusion that she, like Vicki, had jumped to quite independently. Though he had allowed them to go on believing it, of course. She shrugged. 'It was all in a good cause,' she said.

He nodded. 'I knew you'd understand.' Then he gestured to the grey-haired woman at his elbow and drew her forward towards Terri. 'Allow me, belatedly, to introduce you to my mother, Donna Rosaria. *Mamma*—you will remember Vicki's sister Terri. She was at Vicki and Ruggero's wedding, of course.'

Warm brown eyes smiled into hers. 'Of course I remember you. As you are our guest on the island—and Vicki's sister—I should have invited you here long ago.' She made a face, requesting forbearance. 'But things were a little awkward—I hope you'll forgive me. I'm delighted to welcome you now to my home.'

Gratefully, Terri shook her hand, seeing in the strong lines of the woman's face an echo of her eldest son. Perhaps, she found herself thinking, it was not inconceivable that Donna Rosaria had, from time to time, made her presence felt with her young, inexperienced daughter-in-law. But she sensed also that her influence would undoubtedly have been a positive one. 'I'm delighted to be here,' she replied.

They were interrupted as a small, chubby figure appeared between them and tugged for attention at her grandmother's skirt. '*Nonna, Nonna!*'

As the woman bent to scoop the child into her arms, suddenly Vicki was beside them, looking relaxed and happy for once, all the lines of strain vanished from her face. She glanced from her sister to her daughter. 'It's time this young lady was introduced properly to her aunt Terri,' she smiled. And Terri laughed delightedly as big green eyes were turned on her and the introduction was duly made.

She smiled at Vicki. 'She's even prettier than her

photographs.'

Vicki smiled back proudly at her. 'She's gorgeous, isn't she?'

Then Ruggero joined them and addressed himself earnestly to his sister-in-law. 'Vicki's been telling me all about the concern you showed over the past few days. I'd just like you to know that I appreciate that.'

'Don't mention it. I'm just glad that the three of you are back together again. That's the most important thing.' Terri smiled at him, taking in the mild, handsome features, the sensitive brown eyes—and suddenly she sensed that she had been wrong that time she had so peevishly described him to Angelo as weak. That Ruggero, the younger, more impressionable one, should at times have allowed himself to be influenced by his more forceful, dynamic older cousin was really scarcely surprising. Angelo would not be an easy influence to ignore.

But maybe, like Vicki, Ruggero was growing up. Beneath the sensitivity, she could see signs of the Montefalcone toughness showing through. Somehow she had a feeling that Ruggero would prove himself a good husband for Vicki in the end.

Vicki cut in now, 'We both hope you'll come and stay with us for a few days before you leave.'

But Terri smiled and shook her head. 'I wouldn't dream of it!' she protested. 'You and Ruggero need to be on your own—and there's really nothing to keep me here any more.' As she said it, she felt a sudden sharp pain twist in her breast—and found herself glancing in Angelo's direction. There were still a

couple of things left for her to do. She had to thank
Angelo properly for the trouble he had gone to to
bring Ruggero back. And—she winced at the
thought—she had to say goodbye to him.

But, even as she gathered herself inwardly for the
task, she suddenly stopped dead in her tracks. The
spot where he had been standing just a moment before
was completely empty now. Angelo was no longer
there.

As Laura once more claimed the attention of the
little group, Terri spun round anxiously, her eyes
searching the room. But there was no trace of him.
Like a puff of incense, he had disappeared.

For a moment she checked herself. What was she
getting in such a panic about? He had probably just
gone out of the room and would walk back in again
any minute now. But some sixth sense was warning
her otherwise as she remembered what he had told her
back at the farm. 'When the time comes, they just fly
away. Like me, the falcons hate goodbyes.'

Her heart was hammering. She couldn't let him do
it. She had to stop him somehow.

'Excuse me.' With a curt nod to the others, she
turned and walked smartly across the drawing-room
and out into the hall, and glanced quickly right and
left down the corridors that ran off to either side.
Then, half-way to the open front door, she heard the
low growl of a car outside, and her heart went still
inside her chest.

She almost ran the short distance to the door, but
she was too late. Already, the big car was reversing

out into the drive, turning, heading away towards the gates.

Numbly, Terri watched the oblivious dark profile behind the wheel and resisted the urge to run after him. Somehow she managed to choke back the almost frantic longing to call out and beg him to stop. It was just as he had warned her it would be. He was leaving without a backward glance.

With a vast plummet of yearning that almost tore her soul apart, she stood silently in the doorway and watched until the car disappeared from sight.

CHAPTER NINE

'LOOKS like that's the end of the summer. It'll be winter again before we know it!'

As Terri dived into the hallway of the Kentish Town block of flats where she lived, shaking her dripping umbrella and pausing to wipe her sodden feet on the mat, she pulled a face in agreement at the raincoated figure who was on her way out. 'Too right!' she told the red-haired Annabel who lived with her boyfriend in the flat next to hers. 'I make this the third solid day of rain this week!'

Annabel gave an exaggerated shiver. 'I'm just dashing down to the Taj for a takeaway, and then it's a night in front of the box for us.' She grimaced as she stepped out into the blustery street. 'That's if I make it back in one piece!'

Terri smiled wryly to herself as she climbed the stairs to her second-floor flat, grateful that at least she had no need to venture out again tonight. After an unusually chaotic Friday afternoon at the insurance office where she was working now, and the customary uncomfortable ride home on the Northern Line, she was feeling, like Annabel, very much in need of a quiet evening at home. A quiet weekend, come to that.

She frowned and shook her head ruefully as she

stuck her key in the front-door lock. Quiet weekends were something she'd had no shortage of recently. They were becoming a routine part of her life.

Indoors, she picked up the pile of letters lying on the mat, then dropped them quickly on to the hallstand before manoeuvring her still-dripping brolly into the bathroom and peeling off her waterlogged mac.

Through in the bedroom, she paused at the window to glance down at the rainswept suburban scene below. What was it Annabel had said? 'Looks like that's the end of the summer.' Terri pulled the heavy curtains shut and, with a bleak sigh, turned away. The summer had ended for her the moment she had stepped on to the ferry at Santa Pietrina harbour just over two months ago, heading for Catania and her flight back to London. Her original intention of staying on for a while in Italy to extend her holiday had somehow completely lost its appeal. Already, she had been able to feel the chill of winter settling in her heart.

She kicked off her shoes and went through to the kitchen, picking up the pile of mail on the way. First things first—a cup of tea. She switched on the kettle, then sat down and leafed through the envelopes. Amid the usual junk mail and bills there were two that demanded immediate attention. Her heart gave an emotional squeeze at the sight of an Italian stamp. It was from Vicki; she recognised the scrawling, exuberant hand. The other one, with its small, neat writing, was from her mother. She decided to open that one first.

It was full of the usual mundane bits and pieces. Aunt Edna, her mother's sister, was recovering from a heavy cold and the cat was expecting kittens again. But, basically, all was well. Her mother sounded cheerful and at peace with the world. And that was something to be grateful for.

As she slit open Vicki's letter, Terri paused automatically to glance at the postmark. *Napoli*. And she smiled with mixed feelings to herself. It was over a month now since Vicki and Ruggero had moved to Naples, where Ruggero had been put in charge of the local office of Montefalcone Navigation. According to Vicki, it was the best move they could possibly have made. The new job involved much less travelling for Ruggero, and it was clear that they were both feeling much more independent living away from Ruggero's immediate family.

The letter began in her usual breathless fashion—and, as Terri soon discovered, it contained special news. 'Guess what? I'm expecting another baby! Some time around the end of next April. We're both hoping it'll be a boy!'

It was great news. Terri raised her eyes for a moment and gazed into space. Everything was working out perfectly for Vicki and Ruggero, after all. Their new life in Naples had given them the boost they had needed to put the past behind them and make a fresh start. She sighed. And she knew who had been responsible for that.

She bent to read the rest of the letter—all about their beautiful new house, little Laura's new kindergarten and all the new friends they had made, and ending with the usual exhortation to 'come and visit us soon'.

She would, Terri promised to herself as she laid the letter down. She definitely wouldn't wait too long before taking up her sister's invitation. Though the enthusiasm she felt at the prospect was tinged with sadness. Naples wasn't Santa Pietrina. There would be no Angelo.

When Terri had returned to London—the day after Ruggero had returned, and without her seeing Angelo again—it wasn't just the summer that had seemed to come to an abrupt, jarring halt. Some newly kindled spark in her had died as well, though at first she had struggled to keep it alive. With all the optimism she could muster, she had hoped—even prayed—that every knock on the door, every shrill of the phone, every letter that dropped through the letterbox might have Angelo on the other end. But her prayers had been answered with a resounding silence.

Little by little, she had stopped even hoping to hear from him. It was perfectly clear that when he had turned his back on her and driven away that afternoon, like the falcons when they flew away from the farm, he had no intention of retracing his steps. Though she had found some consolation in the belief that one day, sooner or later, she was almost bound to see him again, if not as a lover, at least as a distant relative, on Santa Pietrina, when she went to visit Vicki and Ruggero.

The news of her sister's move to Naples—though she had been happy for Vicki—had come as something of a personal blow. Now there was no cause, ever again, for her to set foot on Santa Pietrina. And, in all probability, she would never see Angelo again.

In the unutterable distress she had felt at the prospect,

she had wondered, masochistically, if that exact conclusion might not have been very much in Angelo's mind when he had given Ruggero the Naples job. Whatever bond had briefly existed between her and him had thus been irrevocably broken, leaving them free to fly their separate ways. That magical evening at the Casa Grande and the moment of tender passion on the beach were all they were ever destined to share.

A sudden sharp tap on the front door brought her abruptly back to the present. Dropping Vicki's letter on the kitchen table, she hurried to answer it.

It was Annabel, in dripping raincoat, carrying a plastic bag of something that smelt distinctly Indian. She grinned at Terri. 'Sorry to bother you,' she began. 'I meant to ask you when I saw you downstairs. But could I possibly borrow your tape-recorder, just for tonight? There's a concert on the radio we want to record, and ours is on the blink.'

'Of course.' Terri was only too happy to oblige. Annabel and her boyfriend were good neighbours, always more than willing to do favours themselves. 'Come in,' she invited, 'while I get it for you.'

'I won't, if you don't mind.' Annabel shook her head and held up the plastic bag in her hand. 'I want to get back before the vindaloo gets cold.'

Terri smiled over her shoulder as she went through to the lounge to unplug the radio-recorder that sat on the shelf unit behind the sofa. 'Not much danger of that,' she joked, 'if it's anything like as hot as the last vindaloo I had from the Taj!' She came back and handed the recorder to Annabel. 'Here you are,' she smiled.

'There's no hurry to bring it back.'

'Thanks a lot.' Annabel smiled back. 'But I'll definitely get it back to you tomorrow.' As she turned away, she threw Terri a wink. 'It's a Bon Jovi concert—Benny's favourite. He'd be ever so disappointed if we didn't get it on tape.'

Terri watched her go, feeling a sudden stab of envy at the fond expression on Annabel's face as she hurried back to her own flat, and Benny. She closed the door and went back into the lounge. The world seemed full of happy couples tonight—Vicki and Ruggero, Annabel and Benny. While she had never felt so desperately alone.

As a sudden wave of bleakness swept over her, she sank down on the sofa and closed her eyes. If only their paths had never crossed at all and she had never learned to love him, never dared to hope. If only he had not swept into her life, pausing just long enough to pluck her heart from her breast before sweeping uncaringly out of it again.

Suppressing a sigh, she half turned round and glanced at the shelf unit at her back. Then, sadly, she let her gaze fall on the little purple leather hood with the pink and blue plumes that had sat there ever since her return. Khan's hood. With a clench of emotion, she reached for it. The hood the falcon had worn that day that Angelo had taken her to see it fly. She touched the soft plumes—his goodbye gift. Then she held it tremblingly against her face as aching tears began to fall.

All at once she was sobbing, endless, helpless, heart-wrenching sobs. Weeping, mourning, for a lost love that had never been hers.

Next morning, Terri got up early and gave herself a good talking to. This hopeless, senseless grief was doing her no good at all.

She cooked herself a substantial breakfast, then, as she ate it, she wrote out a list. 'Things To Do', she wrote at the top, then jotted down, 'see about evening classes', 'buy new shoes', 'cook something special for dinner tonight'. She would keep herself busy, seek out distractions and somehow drive him from her head.

For once, too, she decided to dress up. Recently, at weekends, she had taken to slouching around in jeans. Today she pulled out from her wardrobe a slim black skirt, cream cashmere polo-neck and burgundy jacket. Then she twisted her hair into a sleek knot at the back of her head and regarded her reflection with lifting spirits.

He was probably, right this minute, relaxing at the Casa Grande with some glamorous, adoring member of his harem. She, Terri, would be the very last person on his mind. She slung her black leather bag over her shoulder and headed determinedly for the door. Well, from now on, she vowed, he would be the very last person on hers!

The strategy seemed to work. The woebegone figure of the past few weeks was suddenly transformed into an apparently self-possessed young woman with a deliberately defiant spring in her step. She spent the morning shopping, then treated herself to a sit-down lunch at a local coffee-shop before picking up a video for her evening's entertainment and heading back home again.

She would spend what was left of the afternoon, she decided, writing a long letter of congratulation to Vicki—plus a letter to her mother as well—then sit down and study the literature on evening classes that she had collected from the local library. She smiled a smile of self-congratulation as she stowed away inside the fridge the extravagant fillet steak and chocolate gateau she had bought for tonight. She was doing an outstandingly good job of rehabilitating herself.

And now, before anything else, she would treat herself to a long, lazy bath.

But she was just settling down among the bubbles when the doorbell rang. Terri cursed quietly beneath her breath. It was probably only Annabel, come to return the tape-recorder—and she was sorely tempted to ignore it and just stay where she was. But as it rang again, a little more insistently this time, she rose reluctantly from the steamy, scented water and grabbed her long blue towelling robe from the door. Then, tugging the belt tight at her waist, she hurried to the door.

She pulled the door open with a polite protest on her lips. 'You really shouldn't have bothered . . .' she began. But the words petered off into a stunned silence as she saw standing before her, not her next-door neighbour at all, but a tall, dark-haired man in an immaculate blue suit.

Her heart slammed against her ribs. She swallowed.

'Hello, Teresa,' he said.

In the pallid early autumn light that filtered through

the stairwell window, he looked incongruously sun-tanned, incongruously dark. And above all, she thought with a kind of anguish, quite incongruously handsome, like some exotic bird of paradise that had temporarily strayed from its native patch. She continued to stare at him, speechless, feeling her newly acquired self-possession start to come apart at the seams.

He raised one dark eyebrow and smiled at her. 'What's the matter, Teresa? Aren't you going to ask me in?'

'Of course.' She stepped back hurriedly, pulling the robe closed around her throat, self-consciously aware that the words had come out in a strangled croak.

Angelo walked past her into the tiny hall, then paused to glance down at her with a frown. 'I haven't caught you at an awkward moment, I trust?'

'Of course not.' She shook her head and met his eyes, somehow sensing in the query some suspicion of the presence of another man. A vivid sensation went through her at that. Part resentment—why should he care?—and part a quite illogical anxiety to assure him that nothing could be further from the truth. With an almost apologetic half-smile, she indicated her bare feet and scanty attire. 'I was just about to have a bath,' she explained. Then, hastily regathering her poise, she ushered him through into the lounge. 'Please make yourself comfortable. Take a seat.'

He sat on the edge of the sofa, while she poised herself in an armchair nearby. And there was an aura of strangers confronting one another as he told her, 'You're looking well.'

'Yes, thank you. I've been fine.' She looked across into the unblinking black eyes and felt her heart squeeze to nothingness inside her breast. What if, instead of this polite verbal parrying, she were to confront him with the truth? Confess that she had not been fine at all? That she had missed him and mourned him with an agony of despair that at times had riven her very soul? That this mask of composure he saw now was nothing but a thin and meaningless disguise?

Instead she said, 'You're looking well too.'

He smiled, his eyes on her face, then he sat back in his seat and let his gaze wander round the room. 'So this is where you live? I've often wondered what it was like.'

And why on earth would he do that? she wondered almost harshly, discounting the pleasantry. She said nothing, just toyed, almost unconsciously, with the loose tie-end of her blue towelling belt.

Angelo told her, 'You've done it up nicely. Just as I'd expect.'

He was wearing a plain white shirt—a sharp, clean contrast against the dark blue suit—and a navy and burgundy striped tie. As he leaned back against the cushions and stretched one arm along the back of the sofa, a gesture at once casual and faintly authoritative, Terri was suddenly transported back to that first confrontation at the Casa Grande.

Then, too, as she had sat on the huge divan, gratefully sipping chilled mint tea, she had been acutely conscious of his physical presence. And acutely nervous, though for different reasons. She had also, as now, she recalled, suddenly sensing his eyes on her, been somewhat scantily clad. Quite unnecessarily, she adjusted the long robe about her knees. Then, with a clench of emotion, she asked, 'How are things on the island?'

'As ever. Nothing changes much on Santa Pietrina.' He smiled.

'I suppose it's still like summer there?'

'It is less hot than before. The weather is pleasant at this time of year.'

'And the falcons?' Suddenly her eye had been caught by the little purple leather hood with the pink and blue plumes that sat on the shelf behind his head. 'Have they gone yet?' she wanted to know.

'The chicks, you mean?'

She nodded.

'The last one flew away just a couple of days before I left.' As he spoke, Angelo dropped his arm from the back of the sofa and leaned towards her slightly. 'Teresa——'

But before he could go on she found herself cutting in, a jarringly hostile edge to her voice, 'Angelo, why are you here?' She straightened and stared at him, resentment in every line of her face as all the painful memories of that last visit to the farm suddenly came flooding back. That was when he had spelled it out to her that they had no place in each other's lives. And the memory was like a knife in her heart. 'Presumably,' she told him, her tone aggressive, stiff with sarcasm, 'you haven't come all this way just to indulge in banal conversation with me?'

His eyes swept her face. 'No.'

'Then what are you doing here?'

She waited for him to say that he was in London on business, that he had only stopped by to see her as a gesture of common courtesy. In which case, she silently vowed, she would tell him he need not have bothered and politely invite him to be on his way. Though quite illogically, at the same time, she was inwardly steeling herself against the wash of disappointment that explanation would bring.

The black eyes surveyed her for a moment with uncharacteristic hesitation. He said at last, with a faint inflection, 'I came because I have something to say to you.'

'To me? What?' Terri felt a sudden flash of concern at the unexpected sombre note in his voice. Had he come with some news of Vicki? Was something wrong?

But it was nothing like that. He touched his tie. 'If you want to know the truth, I've missed you,' he said.

For a moment Terri just gaped at him, scarcely able to believe her ears. Then, suddenly, something inside her snapped. '*Missed* me!' she exclaimed. Indignantly she leapt to her feet. 'Surely you don't seriously expect me to believe that?'

He eyed her. 'And why would you disbelieve it?' he asked.

'Because it's utterly preposterous!' she accused. 'If you'd missed me, you'd have got in touch. At the very least, you would have written!'

Angelo said quite calmly, 'I did write.'

Just for a fleeting second then, Terri was thrown. Then she folded her arms across her chest and glared intrepidly down at him. 'No, you didn't! You didn't write once.'

Very slowly, his eyes on her face, Angelo rose to stand in front of her. 'In the course of the past few minutes, you have accused me twice of being a liar.' He held her eyes, then, quite unexpectedly, he smiled. 'But I have to tell you, Teresa, you're wrong. I did write, several times. Only I never sent the letters—I tore them up.' He made a face. 'I was on the point of phoning a hundred times. I even got as far as dialling your number once. Then, at the very last minute, I hung up.'

Dumbstruck, Terri stared at him. Could what he was saying possibly be true?

'Do you believe me?'

In spite of a lingering doubt, she nodded. Why would he bother to invent such a lie?

With a twist of a smile, he came towards her and laid his hands lightly on her shoulders. He told her, 'You look as bewildered as I've been feeling for the past two months. And feeling bewildered,' he assured her wryly, 'is not a state of mind I'm particularly accustomed to.' He paused. 'And the fault, *mia cara* Teresa, is entirely yours.'

'Mine?' Terri stared back at him foolishly, her heart skittering wildly inside her breast. At that moment she was entirely incapable of anything approaching rational thought, let alone of figuring out what he was trying to say to her. All she knew were the piercing dark eyes, burning like rods into her face, and the touch of his fingers, like fire, scorching through the thin towelling robe. 'I don't know what you mean,' she mumbled.

'I mean, *cara* Teresa, that for the past two and a half

months I have thought of little else but you—day and night, night and day. In spite of determined efforts on my part to drive all thoughts of you away.'

As she frowned, he dropped one hand from her shoulder and tilted her chin with his fingertips, his other hand slipping down to hold her lightly by the arm. 'When the obsession started—which was more or less that first time you came to my house—I told myself I'd shake myself free of it just as soon as you'd left the island. You will remember,' he pointed out with a faintly self-mocking ring in his voice, 'that I was not exactly at pains to encourage you to stay . . .'

Quite involuntarily, Terri winced. She had no need to be reminded of that.

He leaned and kissed her on the forehead, a gesture of apology and reassurance. 'After you'd left, however, the obsession simply grew.' He straightened and looked down at her, his expression serious. 'What I'm trying to tell you, Teresa—and this I would never say to you unless I was absolutely sure . . .' He paused and raised one eyebrow at her. 'The truth is, Teresa, *mia cara*, I've fallen hopelessly in love with you.'

'Love?' Incredulously, she echoed the word.

'Yes, *love*,' he affirmed. Then he sighed and narrowed his eyes at her before asking, 'Tell me how long you were on the island?'

Terri knew exactly. 'Eight days.'

He smiled. 'Now tell me,' he went on, 'is it possible to fall so deeply in love in so short a time?'

Perfectly possible, she thought. But she couldn't bring herself to say it. Instead, she told him, 'I really don't know.'

'Don't you?' Angelo gave her a long look. 'Well, I can assure you, it is.'

She continued to stare at him, feeling her whole being torn in two—longing to throw herself into his arms and tell him that she loved him too, yet, deep down, still scarcely able to take in the hugeness of his revelation—and driven by some fearful need to query it, to challenge it. 'So why,' she enquired tensely, 'did it take you so long to come and tell me?'

The fingers around her arm tightened slightly. 'Believe me, Teresa, staying away from you was hell—the worst kind of hell I've ever endured.' A deep frown appeared between his brows. 'But I had to be absolutely sure. Nothing even remotely like this has ever happened to me before.'

Terri could see from the light that shone in his eyes that every word he said was true. It was a light at once nakedly revealing yet unflickeringly fierce and strong. As he added, 'I love you, Teresa. It would have been sheer madness for me to have stayed away a moment more,' she felt the dam of emotion give way inside her and helpless tears rise to her eyes.

'Oh, lord!' She just stood there like a child as the joy, the anguish, the relief went sweeping through her in a torrent of release. Her voice breaking, she told him in what was part an accusation and part a simple expression of relief, 'I thought I'd never see you again!'

'Teresa, *tesoro* . . .' Suddenly his arms were round her, holding her close. He was kissing her hair. '*Ti amo, tesoro*. I love you,' he told her. 'Forgive me, my love.'

With a little whimper, she clung to him. 'Oh, Angelo, I thought I'd die!' Then she looked up at last into the fiery dark eyes. 'I love you with all my soul.'

The next moment his lips were on hers as he crushed her to him with an aching moan. '*Tesoro!*' he murmured. And she could feel her senses ignite as his mouth moved hungrily against hers, urgent, sensuous. And she shivered with a raw, fierce clench of desire as his hand moved round inside her robe to caress the warm, excited swell of her breast. It is not possible, she thought weakly, to want a man this much.

But then, before she had time to think another thought, in one smooth movement Angelo had swept her into his arms. He looked down at her with a roguish smile. 'I have just one question to ask you before I carry you through to the bedroom,' he said.

A willing captive held against his chest, Terri smiled back at him. Her heart was hammering. 'And what question is that?'

He kissed her, his expression grown suddenly serious. 'It is the question I came all this way to ask. Teresa, I want you to marry me.'

'Marry?' The hammering in her chest had stopped. The silence that descended was deafening.

He waited. 'Well?'

Terri took a deep breath. 'I thought you said you weren't ready for the restrictions of marriage?'

Angelo nodded, acknowledging the remark he had made that evening over dinner. 'But I was wrong,' he promised her now. 'I'm more than ready. I love you and I want you to be my wife.' Then he smiled and kissed her nose. 'We go not one step beyond this spot unless the answer is yes.'

'In that case, what else can I say?' The flippant, teasing response fell from her lips almost in defence of the deep, overwhelming happiness that had, quite suddenly, invaded her heart, and which shone, uninhibited, from her eyes. She hugged him with all the love in her soul. 'Of course I'll marry you,' she said.

She was glad they had waited. Making love for the very first time on the double bed in her Kentish Town flat might have lacked some of the outward glamour of a warm, star-canopied Sicilian beach—but now there was a special bond between them that had not existed before. More than passion. More than love. A deep, significant sense of commitment, an intermingling of their two lives.

As Angelo laid her on the eiderdown and began to undo the belt at her waist, she reached out for a moment gently to caress his face. This is the man, she told herself with a growing sense of wonder and awe, who will live with me and make love to me for all the remaining days of my life. She closed her eyes as the robe fell open and he bent to kiss her upturned breasts. My first and last lover, she thought with a sigh. The only man I could ever love.

Then he was lying alongside her, naked and warm, his body moulded against hers as he kissed her and caressed her and prepared her to receive his love.

'*Sei bella*,' he whispered against her ear, and she could feel the swift race of her own heart as his lips moved to plant a burning trail of kisses across her shoulders, her collarbone, her neck, the fluttering, nervous pulse in her throat.

His hand swept over her naked body, sending tremors of excitement through her veins as he paused with tantalising thoroughness to graze her swollen nipples with his palms. Then he was travelling on downwards, in a smooth, unhurried caress, to stroke her stomach, the span of her waist, the eager, trembling curve of her hips, then delicately parting her thighs to touch the female core of her.

She gasped, the blood singing in her ears, feeling her breath catch in her throat at the intimacy of his caress, burning in a maelstrom of rising tension as he whipped her senses to fever-pitch.

'Angelo!' She reached out for him, her fingers scraping the muscular shoulders, tangling in the thick, dark hair. One moment more of waiting, she thought, and I shall lose my mind.

With impeccable timing, he came to her, the warm, male hardness of him for a moment pressing urgently against her thigh. Then his mouth was crushing down on hers again, the broad chest lowering against her breasts, and with a murmured, 'Teresa!' in one sure movement he had entered her.

It was a giddy, indescribable sensation to feel him moving inside her. This sense of oneness, this completeness, the surprise, the simplicity of it all. Every atom of her being was all at once focused on the gathering rhythm of their locked bodies, the spiralling pulse of excitement that was drawing them together towards some impossible peak.

She clung to him, feeling the tears rise to her eyes as the momentum of his passion increased, then seemed, deep within her, to break free just as, simultaneously, her own unstoppable crescendo exploded in a thousand incandescent stars.

As the tears of love and release blurred her eyes, she shivered and sighed. I could die right now, she thought, and know that I had touched perfect happiness.

The motor-launch came shimmering out of the heat haze like a great white bird, slicing through the jewel-blue waters of the harbour as it headed for the jetty, twin sheets of foamy, iridescent spray arching outward from its bows.

At the sight of it, Terri's heart gave a lift. She glanced up at the man at her side as he smiled down at her.

'Nearly home now,' he said.

She grinned at him. 'I can scarcely believe it.'

'Well, you'd better believe it.' Angelo leaned down and kissed her. 'From now on, *mia cara* Teresa, this is where you belong.'

The big, elegant motor-launch with the red and gold badge on the prow displaying the Montefalcone coat of arms was already drawing alongside the specially reserved mooring at the end of the jetty where Terri and Angelo were waiting. As it bumped into position, the bearded co-pilot saluted them. '*Benvenuti*! Welcome!' Then he added, darting a swift glance in Terri's direction, 'And congratulations, if I may say so, sir.'

'Thank you.' Angelo grinned in response and Terri felt a flush creep to her cheeks as the man held out his

hand to help her on board with a respectful, '*Venga,
signora!*'

It was going to take her a little time, she guessed, to
grow accustomed to the new form of address!

The red leather of the upholstery was warm from the
autumn sun as she seated herself in the stern, her eyes
on the handsome, sun-tanned face of the man who was
climbing in beside her. My husband, she thought with a
jolt of pride, and glanced down at her hand as the gold
band on her finger momentarily caught the sun. Just two
days ago, in a modest little ceremony in London, she
and Angelo had taken their wedding vows. Only her
mother and Aunt Edna had been present—and a
somewhat dazzled Annabel and Benny.

'I *knew* you'd met some man while you were over in
Sicily!' Annabel had confided. 'And now that I've met
him I can understand why you appeared to be missing
him so much!'

A much grander ceremony lay ahead of them in a few
days' time—in the private chapel of the Casa Grande,
surrounded by the entire Montefalcone clan. Which was
why, at Angelo's insistence, they had stopped off in
Rome for a day to buy the most exquisite wedding dress
Terri had ever set eyes on in her life.

But for now, all that was really on her mind was
returning with Angelo to Santa Pietrina. The island
where it had all begun. The island where they would
spend their future together as man and wife.

Her heart fluttered excitedly as the motor-launch
wheeled in an arc round the harbour and headed back
for the open sea. In just fifteen minutes they would be

home.

As the warm wind whipped through her hair, Angelo reached out to draw her close, his arm around her shoulder, the long, strong fingers laced with her own. Then all at once he glanced up at the sky. 'Look, Teresa!' He pointed. 'They've come to welcome you back!'

As she followed his pointing finger, her heart was suddenly alight with joy. For there above them, like a precious omen of happiness to come, flew a falcon. Swooping and diving. A gold-tipped, shimmering silhouette dancing in the sun.

A Mother's Day Treat

This beautifully packaged set of brand new Romances makes an id[eal] choice of Mother's Day gift.

BLUEBIRDS IN THE SPRIN[G]
Jeanne Allen
THE ONLY MAN
Rosemary Hammond
MUTUAL ATTRACTION
Margaret Mayo
RUNAWAY
Kate Walker

These top authors have been selected for their blend of styles, and with romance the key ingredient to all the storylines, what better way t[o] treat your mother... or even yourself.

Available from February 199[0]
Price £5.40

From: Boots, Martins, John Menzi[es] W.H. Smith, Woolworths and othe[r] paperback stockists.

SOLITAIRE – Lisa Gregory £3.50

Emptiness and heartache lay behind the facade of Jennifer Taylor's glittering Hollywood career. Bitter betrayal had driven her to become a successful actress, but now at the top, where else could she go?

SWEET SUMMER HEAT – Katherine Burton £2.99

Rebecca Whitney has a great future ahead of her until a sultry encounter with a former lover leaves her devastated...

THE LIGHT FANTASTIC – Peggy Nicholson £2.99

In this debut novel, Peggy Nicholson focuses on her own profession... Award-winning author Tripp Wetherby's fear of flying could ruin the promotional tour for his latest blockbuster. Rennie Markell is employed to cure his phobia, whatever it takes!

These three new titles will be out in bookshops from February 1990.

W★RLDWIDE

Available from Boots, Martins, John Menzies, W.H. Smith, Woolworths and other paperback stockists.

2 NEW TITLES FOR JANUARY 1990

Mariah by Sandra Canfield is the first novel in a sensational quartet of sisters in search of love... Mariah's sensual and provocative behaviour contrasts enigmatically with her innocent and naive appearance... Only the maverick preacher can recognise her true character and show her the way to independence and true love.

£2.99

Faye is determined to make a success of the farm she has inherited – but she hadn't accounted for the bitter battle with neighbour, Seth Carradine, who was after the land himself. In desperation she turns to him for help, and an interesting bargain is struck.

Kentucky Woman by Casey Douglas, bestselling author of Season of Enchantment. **£2.99**

W🌐RLDWIDE

Available from Boots, Martins, John Menzies, W.H. Smith, Woolworths and other paperback stockists.